MURDER ON
THE YACHT

THE LT. VALCOUR SERIES

MURDER ON THE YACHT

RUFUS KING

A Lt. Valcour Mystery

WILDSIDE PRESS

PART ONE

CHAPTER ONE

MR. HEDGLIN IS QUEER

The yacht *Crusader*'s departure was overshadowed with prophetic trouble. She rode at anchor in the East River off the foot of 23rd Street, a glistening and expensive ship, with New York's night sheaves of static rockets on her starboard bow and Brooklyn, more quietly spectacular, at her left.

Captain Nils Jorgensen, competently stuffed into smart blue serge, was taking the air upon her bridge, and Mr. Burke, the steward, a pallid-faced man and somberly dark-eyed (no amount of sun or wind at sea had ever roughed or tanned him) was taking it with him. Night traffic on the polished wet black river was slack and a Sound steamer, like an overdressed and too important lady, was the only craft found going by.

Mr. Burke, in addition to taking the air, was worried. "Wouldn't you know it?" he said.

Captain Jorgensen was a stolid and forthright man. He had small patience with rhetorical questions, and none at all with any vagaries in speech. He said: "Know what?"

"The Lithia"

"The what?"

"The Lithia water. It isn't here."

"Why isn't it here?"

"It didn't come."

Captain Jorgensen eyed a watch on his strong broad wrist. Above the watch's leather strap was a thin gold bracelet, linked, and from which dangled a heart-shaped locket. In the locket was a diminutive photograph of a Norwegian girl named Olga. Olga was dead. He said: "If it is not here in an hour, we will sail without Lithia water."

"He'll raise hell."

"Who will raise hell?"

"Mr. Luke will."

Mr. Wharton Luke was the owner's brother-in-law.

"That has nothing to do with me. My orders are to sail at one minute past midnight." Captain Jorgensen, while continuing to take the air, kept a professional and agate-blue eye on two sailors by the anchor winch up forward on the deck below him. "It will shortly be time for Mr. Jones to be on deck." (Mr. Jones was the first officer.) "I will thank you, Steward, to stop by at his cabin and—"

The sentence was broken off by a: "*Crusader*, ahoy!" The hail had come from a launch on the wet jet river.

"The Lithia water!" said Mr. Burke, and ran down the ladder to the main deck and headed for the accommodation ladder's platform on the starboard rail.

He was almost feverishly glad that it had come (the Lithia water), as Mr. Luke had a special and oddly disagreeable type of hell when he raised it. Subtle. That was it: a rather incomprehensible and subtle type of hell. Mr. Burke stared with his somber eyes down at the launch. It didn't look like the kind of launch that would bring Lithia water.

"The yacht *Crusader*?" a quiet and efficient sounding voice was calling up at him. It wasn't the sort of voice that would come bringing Lithia water.

"Yes," Mr. Burke said. "Have you got it?"

"I beg your pardon?"

"Have you got the Lithia water?"

"This is a police launch."

"Oh." Mr. Burke's somber eyes were suddenly queer and sharp. Several trifling peccadilloes of recent years loomed largely. "Beg pardon, sir. You wish to board us?"

"I would like," the quiet voice went on, "to speak with Mr. Anthony Bettle. He is the owner, is he not?"

"Yes sir"

"He is on board?"

"Yes, sir. Mr. Bettle is in his quarters."

"Thank you."

A man mounted the steps of the accommodation ladder and stepped onto the deck. He was a tall, well-built man of middle age, dressed in conservative tweeds. He stared almost absently for a moment at Burke, and then said: "If you will be good enough to request Mr. Bettle to see me? I am Lieutenant Valcour from the detective division at headquarters."

"May I show you into the saloon, sir?"

"Thank you, I will wait here."

"Very good, sir."

Valcour leaned against teak railing and watched a tall bulk of a man in uniform coming along the deck toward him.

"I am Captain Jorgensen," the bulk said.

"My name is Valcour, Captain; Lieutenant Valcour of the detective division."

"Your business, Lieutenant, is with Mr. Bettle?"

"Yes, Captain."

"I trust it will not be lengthy." Captain Jorgensen pointedly examined his wrist watch. "We are sailing in fifty-five minutes."

"I see no reason why I shall not be finished by then."

Captain Jorgensen had the usual amount of healthy curiosity possessed by the normal male. He wanted to ask point-blank what business it was which had caused a police officer to board the *Crusader*, but there were lots of things you didn't do point-blank on yachts. That was the main trouble with yachts. They were the only type vessel afloat on which the owners were so intimately underfoot and, like all soft berths, a yacht's captaincy had its disadvantages. He said: "I am glad of that. Mr. Bettle is a particular man, not only as to the hour but even to the minute of our sailings. Myself, Lieutenant, I am not given to such acute finenesses, but my job depends upon their observation. You did not by chance see a boat with Lithia water?"

Valcour smiled slightly. "I believe not."

"That is too bad. It is too bad for our steward, Mr. Burke. Mr. Burke ordered it and it did not come. Mr. Luke is going to give him hell."

"Mr. Luke?"

"He is Mr. Bettle's brother-in-law. He is a funny man, and I do not mean by that that he makes you laugh." One of the point-blank things you didn't do on yachts was to comment on the owner's guests. No matter. This police lieutenant was impermanent. He would be here and gone, and what was said to him here would be quickly gone with him when he went. A man had to talk, and Captain Jorgensen's sole conception of the art of conversation was an immediate exposure of whatever happened to be on his mind at the moment when he opened his mouth. "Mr. Luke will say things that sound like nonsense, and the next day you will remember them and they will make sense. If things do not go right to suit him, he will make a remark which you will think nothing at all about until several hours later, and then it will begin to fester up inside of you like a sore. If that Lithia water does not come before we sail, I am sorry for poor Burke."

"Mr. Luke sounds interesting. Whom else have you on board, Captain?"

Captain Jorgensen enjoyed tabulations. They were so pleasingly orderly. He said: "There are the owner's wife and son. She is a very quiet woman and not nosy. It would astonish you, Lieutenant, the nosiness which a woman can develop on board a ship. The son is meek. He will soon be twenty-one years old, and his name is John. I have already told you about Mr. Bettle's brother-in-law, Wharton Luke. As guests, there are a Mr. Horatio Barlowe and his daughter Freda. He is a very stout man with a jolly smile, and she has red hair. With them is a Miss Singlestar, who is a companion for Miss Barlowe. Then there is a young man by the name of Moore. Peter Moore, I think it is. There is lastly, Lieutenant, a Miss Carlotta Balfé."

"Carlotta Balfé. That is a curious name."

"She is a curious woman. I cannot make her out. She looks a good many things that she does not tell."

Valcour said thoughtfully: "And that is all?"

"That is all. They are all aboard now. There was one other gentleman who came, but I understand he is now gone and does not come back."

"I see."

The wash from a passing tug slapped sloshing hollowly against the *Crusader*'s plates as Mr. Burke materialized himself beside them like a clever and silent trick. He said to Valcour: "Mr. Bettle will see you at once, sir. If you will come with me, please, to his quarters?"

"You will pardon me, Captain?"

"Yes, Lieutenant." Captain Jorgensen took another significant look at his watch. "We are sailing—I remind you again of it—in fifty minutes."

"I shall bear it in mind."

They went aft (Burke and Valcour) along an empty deck to a door which led directly into the sitting room of Mr. Bettle's suite. Burke held it open, and Valcour stepped over its combing.

Anthony Bettle was standing: a big, heavy-boned, impressive man with an elderly and strongly lined face that seemed totally unfamiliar with the pleasure of smiling. It interested Valcour to meet the successful rich. He thought of them as a brotherhood linked by a secret and dynamic source of energy, a common flux, that had tempered them to a strength above that of ordinary men. Their foibles alone differentiated them, and Valcour had stopped being astonished at the deliberate and concentrative energy with which a wealthy man would foster his special conceit.

Valcour had personally encountered several such hobbies that had lain outside the ordinary fields of, for example, collecting objects of art or antiquity, the financing of explorations, the backing of scientific, of theatrical, ventures. He knew one man who had had constructed a miniature railway system so intricate and detailed that it had taken three years to complete and had cost a fortune. Another had specialized in the propagation of toads, for the benefit of his own gardens and the gardens of anybody else whom he could bully or impress into being interested. These hobbies had without exception developed into monomanias.

He wondered what Anthony Bettle's was.

Bettle was advancing upon Valcour with his hand extended; like a slow and heavy wind his advance was, with an unconscious effect of strength and exactness of purpose. "Lieutenant Valcour? How do you do. I suppose that your visit is official?"

"Yes, Mr. Bettle. I am here to make some inquiries about a Mr. Waverly Hedglin."

"Sit down, won't you?"

"Thank you."

"I shan't ask you to smoke, as I do not approve of tobacco. I won't offer you a drink, as I disapprove of liquor. I explain both prejudices at once upon meeting anybody, as it saves future embarrassment." There was nothing either overbearing or disagreeable in the making of the statements. There was no doubting their sincerity. "What is the nature of the inquiries, Mr. Valcour?"

"We are worried about Mr. Hedglin. We understand that he planned to sail with you to-night, in company with his nephew, for the West Indies. Is that correct?"

"Yes. Partially. Jumentos Cays, the Ragged Island, is our destination, to be exact. It makes a better base. But that's beside the point. It doesn't matter." Anthony Bettle gave the impression of verbally touching peaks which were only comprehensible to a listener who was familiar with their valleys. "The fact is that Hedglin won't be with us after all. He's ashore. There are times when I think he carries his reserves too far. He's a lawyer, you know, and the whole breed seems to make some sort of a fetish out of secrecy. And I don't like it. He was taken ashore in the tender about two hours ago."

"You are not expecting him to return?"

"No. He stated that he wouldn't return. What are you leading up to, Mr. Valcour?"

"We were puzzled over a report made at headquarters by a taxi driver. The commissioner thought that I ought to investigate it."

"A report about Hedglin?"

"One concerning him. Mr. Hedglin picked the cab up at the dock at the foot of East Twenty-third Street. He told the driver to take him to the vicinity of Times Square and then, after they'd gone a few blocks, he localized his order by telling the man to drive him to the Astor Hotel. When the doorman at the Astor opened the cab door, Mr. Hedglin was no longer inside. There was nothing in the cab but a black overcoat and a derby hat."

Valcour had a curious feeling that Anthony Bettle was giving his mind to something else, to something entirely remote from the odd vanishing of Hedglin. Bettle's whole manner was one of polite disattention. He was not sitting easily in the comfortable chair. His body and his expression were quiet enough, but his thoughts seemed to be racing along some private channel of their own.

"That seems absurd. Why should Hedglin do a thing like that?"

"We don't," Valcour said, "think he did."

CHAPTER TWO

WATER WETS A RUG

It continued to be present (this lack of attention on Anthony Bettle's part) even in the face of what must have been an astonishing and disturbing fact. Important men did not step into taxicabs and then vanish from them, leaving their hats and overcoats behind. But Bettle was not impressed. His interest in the situation remained courteously intelligent, but only to the extent of the subject's surface. The weather itself could not have evoked a more detached or calmly measured attitude as a topic. In spite of all this, he did not miss any pertinent point. He said: "Unless the driver was aware of his identity, how did he know that his fare was Hedglin?"

"He didn't. We found that out from letters in a pocket of the overcoat. They were addressed to Mr. Hedglin. We got in touch at once with his apartment by telephone. His man reported that Mr. Hedglin had left with his nephew for this yacht, so the commissioner thought I had better come here and see you, while they were checking up ashore."

"Checking up how, Mr. Valcour?" The question was on the verge of being academic.

Valcour said: "There are several things they're doing ashore. They've made the driver remember as many points as possible where he had to stop for traffic, or to slow down sufficiently for a man to leave the cab without creating notice. They're checking up at such of those points where a traffic policeman happened to have been stationed, or where the man on beat may have happened to be near by."

"That's an intricate and lengthy job, is it not?"

It was interesting to Valcour that not once had there been a single expression of concern from Anthony Bettle as to any possible disaster that might have happened to Hedglin. He said: "Such a job is largely a matter of established routine. It is done much faster than you think."

"And what is your end of the investigation, Mr. Valcour?" Bettle added: "I mean here."

"I would like to interview Mr. Hedglin's nephew and whoever saw Mr. Hedglin while he was on board. It would help us if we could determine his recent mental attitude. He may have given some verbal intimation of his intention of disappearing, if it should turn out that he did purposely disappear. But that is a theory which is not plausibly tenable."

"Why not?"

"It isn't plausible because if Mr. Hedglin had wanted to disappear he wouldn't have left identifying letters in his coat pocket. He wouldn't have left his coat. He wouldn't have left his hat." Such things, Valcour's manner implied, were simply not done in the best disappearances.

Anthony Bettle's manner was suddenly careful. "You must forgive me," he said, "for leaning toward a simple and not exciting solution. We have Hedglin entering the cab alone and leaving it alone. It is an odd thing to do, if you wish, but Hedglin is a man who carries a great deal on his mind. It might have been done quite involuntarily. I can assure you, from the note he left me, that he was puzzling over a certain matter very deeply."

"Note?" Valcour was immediately alert. "He left without seeing you?"

Anthony Bettle was off again on his private mental race. "I haven't seen Hedglin since three o'clock yesterday afternoon," he said.

It was like sinking gently into cloudy waters—*he left a note*—*I haven t seen Hedglin since three o'clock yesterday afternoon*—and there was Bettle, outwardly serene, busily racing his mind. Valcour said: "Will you tell me what was in the note, please?"

"Certainly. Hedglin said in it that he had suddenly realized the significance of one of the details in an investigation he is conducting for me, and he thought it advisable to go ashore and follow it up at once. He plans to rejoin us by steamer as soon as he has cleared the matter up."

"Was it a long note, Mr. Bettle?"

"Quite long. It was sufficiently detailed."

"I don't understand it. I don't mean the note, I mean the fact that he wrote to you at all, instead of seeing you personally."

"Hedglin is impulsive. Perhaps he felt there wasn't time."

"It generally takes longer to write a thing than it does to say it. I suppose you recognized the handwriting all right?"

"It was typewritten. Hedglin always uses a portable. There was nothing wrong with the signature." Anthony Bettle looked at his watch. "You will not think me rude for pointing out that our sailing time is shortly under forty minutes. You wish to see Peter Moore, Hedglin's nephew. I understand that he and the steward and Miss Carlotta Balfé are the only people who saw Hedglin while he was on board. Perhaps it will even not be necessary, Mr. Valcour, for you to interview them personally. I know that Peter knew nothing of his uncle's sudden intention of not sailing. When I read it to him, the note came as a complete surprise. I am sure that the steward did no more than take Hedglin's bags to his cabin, and Carlotta Balfé's only part in the business was to wave to Hedglin from her deck chair as Hedglin stepped into the tender to be taken ashore." Bettle's gesture implied: *You will save me and yourself all sorts of bother if you simply take my word for these things.*

Valcour was worried. It was a commonplace rule of the police to handle all rich and influential men with gloves except in extreme cases, and there was nothing as yet tangibly extreme in the matter of Hedglin. "Will you permit me to see Mr. Hedglin's cabin?" he said.

"Certainly. Come, I'll show you."

They did not go out on deck. Anthony Bettle led the way through a door opening into a central fore-and-aft passageway. They passed two doors on the right. Bettle opened the third and they entered a comfortably large and well-appointed room. The lights were on. There were two Gladstone bags and a wardrobe suitcase neatly lined against a wall.

"I see that he left his luggage," Valcour said.

"Yes. The steward thought it odd. He carried nothing ashore with him but his briefcase."

Valcour was staring at the center of the rug which covered the floor. He stooped and touched several large damp spots. "It's water," he said. "There has been quite a lot of water spilled recently on this rug." He went over to the room's basin. It was very clean and dry. Racked above it were two glasses and a carafe. The carafe was filled with water.

"Burke may have spilled it when he came in to fill that carafe," Bettle said, and glanced impatiently at his watch.

"Possibly." Valcour smiled and took a small magnifying lens from a vest pocket. "You will forgive me for running true to form?" He studied the carafe through the lens. He turned and said: "I am sorry, Mr. Bettle, but it won't do."

"What won't do, Mr. Valcour?"

There was a discernible tightening in Valcour's attitude. He became quite formal. He said: "I regret advising you that this yacht must not leave our jurisdiction until essential questions concerning Mr. Hedglin's disappearance have been answered to our satisfaction. I am sorry if this inconveniences you."

There was no abrupt about-face, but Bettle's manner became moderately conciliatory. "It isn't a question of convenience, and you mustn't imagine that I'm callous to Hedglin's welfare. I'm not. We're friends. We have been the closest friends for years, and I don't believe there is any man I know more intimately than Hedglin. But I am honestly not worried. I stress again that he had a great deal on his mind."

"May I ask of what nature?"

"It is immaterial." Anthony Bettle was decisive about this. "It concerns a project—one entirely disassociated from my business ventures—that has interested me profoundly for the past two or three years." (Valcour thought: *So that's it—the hobby. It's here again: the almost fanatical eagerness with which a rich man will pursue his hobby*.) "The project is now actively under way. Let me tell you, Mr. Valcour, that I think of little else. I think of it intensely. There are times when, so far as my body is concerned, I find myself going through the routine motions of daily life automatically, but my mind is unaware of what I am doing. Can you understand that? I tell you this because I believe that it is what has happened to Hedglin. He is as deeply involved in this project as myself."

"I quite understand the principle of what you mean, and I agree with it. But in this special instance I am skeptical about the details."

"I don't follow you, Mr. Valcour."

"Well, I dislike the fact that Mr. Hedglin boarded this yacht, and decided suddenly to leave it without having seen you personally. Had you given any instructions that you were not to be disturbed?"

"No. None."

"I can understand the ordinary physical actions of daily life being done automatically, as you pointed out, but it does not seem to me to be a matter of daily routine to take off one's hat and overcoat in a taxicab. Such an action cannot have been the result of habit. Don't you agree with me there?"

Anthony Bettle was again absorbed in his watch. He said absently: "Yes, that is so."

"I can understand Mr. Hedglin's leaving his luggage behind, but I cannot understand the amount and the location of the water that has been spilled on this rug, nor can I understand that that carafe shows no fingerprints. Then there is one other thing about this whole business that I understand least of all."

Bettle's "What?" was impatiently sharp.

"The odd fact that while he was waiting with the watchman on the dock for the taxicab to drive up, Mr. Hedglin deliberately took his hat off and fanned his face."

CHAPTER THREE

A YACHT SAILS STRANGELY

Bettle said: "Look here, Mr. Valcour, I'm not trying to be offensive. I just want to be clear and quick. I've given you my interpretation of this business of Hedglin's and I'm personally satisfied with it. You and the police department are at liberty to entertain any other interpretation that you like, but I don't intend postponing our sailing just because Hedglin stood on a dock and fanned his face with his hat."

Valcour flushed slightly. "The incident is not as trivial as you imply."

"That is again a matter of personal interpretation, and as I told you I am not trying to be offensive, but there is no time to mince words. You claim that Hedglin disappeared ashore. All right, then, the proper place to look for him is ashore. This yacht sails in twenty minutes."

Valcour thought for a moment, staring at Anthony Bettle, wondering as to the nature of the compelling "project" which made Bettle so nervously indifferent to the possible fate of a man whom he admitted to be a lifelong friend, wondering at this willful blinding of himself on Bettle's part to facts that seemed so dangerously significant. He said : "As you feel so strongly about it, Mr. Bettle, I dislike exerting my authority without first communicating with the commissioner. Would you care to come ashore with me while I telephone?"

"We can telephone from here. I was about to suggest it. I will talk with the commissioner myself."

Anthony Bettle was suddenly like a large and shepherding dog intent upon herding Valcour from the room. He was almost physically enveloping, even over Valcour, who was himself a large and powerful man.

"You are connected by a telephone cable?" Valcour said.

"No. We have a radio-telephone installation on board. I find it convenient."

They left the cabin and continued forward along the passage, the door at whose end opened directly into the main saloon. There was a woman sitting on a lounge in the saloon's corner. Her lips were a red wide slash in whiteness and her eyes were as black as her hair. She gave the singular impression of having been done modernly in caricature, and the flame chiffon of her dress was violent against the tapestry of the couch. She sat quite still and stared fixedly at Anthony Bettle, who ignored her entirely and who was, with vague shepherding motions, propelling Valcour through the saloon and out onto the deck. The woman had looked once very directly at Valcour just before they reached the door. He thought that her lips had smiled faintly.

A ladder led them up to the boat deck and they entered the wireless room, which was just abaft the charthouse. Bettle said at once to the operator: "Get me the police commissioner. Try headquarters first, and if he isn't there find out where I can get in touch with him. I want him right away."

"Yes, sir."

Valcour sensed it in the operator's manner, in the faint pulsations of the yacht's powerful Diesel engines, in the very air: that alert, intangible expectancy which energizes a ship during those last and always subconsciously exciting moments before she puts to sea.

Anthony Bettle was no longer overpowering and shepherding him. Bettle was overpowering and shepherding the wireless operator. And Burke, the steward, was suddenly standing in the doorway and saying to Valcour: "Another police launch has just come alongside, Lieutenant. The officer in charge says he has a report for you."

"Then get him up here quickly," Bettle said.

"Yes, sir."

Bettle was momentarily nasty. "We'll have the whole department here before we leave." He turned to the wireless operator. "Is that call through yet?"

The wireless man continued to do things with the intricacies of his panel. "Coming through now, sir."

Bettle said with an irritated intenseness to Valcour: "You don't understand this one bit."

"I appreciate the annoyance, naturally."

"It isn't annoyance. It's more important than just annoyance. There are very definite calculations. We must sail on the minute."

(…"Police headquarters? The yacht *Crusader* talking. Mr. Anthony Bettle, the owner, wishes to be connected with the commissioner at once. The matter is urgently important. Beg pardon?…")

"The calculations involve your sailing time, Mr. Bettle?" Valcour was puzzled.

"Yes. Operator, is that call through?"

"In one moment, sir."

"It's an outrage, Mr. Valcour, to have the culmination of several years of intensive preparation jeopardized by—Well?" The word was an angry bullet shot at a police sergeant standing in the deck doorway.

Sergeant McGuire was rigidly at attention. He was enormously impressed not only with the yacht, but by his being on her. He included Anthony Bettle's back in his salute (Bettle had gone to the wireless phone) and said to Valcour: "The place where Hedglin left the cab has been located, Lieutenant."

(…"Yes? Headquarters? Commissioner's office? Beg your pardon, sir. Mr. Bettle is right here.—The commissioner, Mr. Bettle."…) Valcour said: "Yes, Sergeant?"

"Officer Muldoon was on duty, Lieutenant, at Broadway and Forty-fifth Street when he sees this cab stop for cross traffic and this bird Hedglin hops out. He notices him because it's a cold night and he ain't got no hat or coat on, and besides which he seems nervous and in a bad hurry. Well, Muldoon thinks it's some bird beating his fare, and then he thinks maybe it's some nut or some souse, and he's on his way over to investigate when the lights change and the cab's gone on ahead and the man's lost in the crowd."

(…"Commissioner? Bettle speaking—Anthony Bettle—yes—yes… Now see here, Commissioner…")

"Any description of the man, Sergeant?"

"No, sir. He ducked right into the crowd. Just that he was tall and lanky and was carrying a briefcase."

"Sounds like Hedglin."

("…and furthermore, Commissioner—damn this static—I said furthermore, in ten minutes it is vitally essential that we sail, so…")

"What did Muldoon mean, Sergeant, about the man seeming nervous and in a bad hurry?"

"Why just that, Lieutenant."

"All right. What I meant was: did Hedglin seem nervously hurried to get to some place, or was he trying to escape from something?"

"Sure Muldoon said that outside of the fact that this souse…"

(…"Very well, Commissioner. It's an odd suggestion, but I appreciate it…")

Captain Jorgensen, clearly dominating the room's cross-currents, cut through them by standing in the open doorway and saying: "We have five minutes left exactly, Mr. Bettle. Are there any changes of sailing orders?"

"One minute, please, Commissioner—no, Captain, we will sail on the dot—You will speak to him yourself, Commissioner? He is here.—Mr. Valcour, please speak with the commissioner."

It was immensely confusing.

Valcour took the phone and the commissioner's voice came clearly, with brief intervals of unintelligibility caused by the brittle crash of atmospherics: "...naturally we wish to humor Mr. Bettle as much as possible...most determined on sailing at once...your opinion?"

"My opinion," Valcour said, "is that the key to Mr. Hedglin's strange actions lies right here on this yacht."

"I agree with you. I suggested to Mr. Bettle that, inasmuch as he insists on sailing immediately, you sail with him, too. We will cover the shore end here. It will only mean a brief cruise on the yacht and a return by steamer. The department cannot have the disappearance of two noted men on its hands in such short order."

(The commissioner was referring to the disappearance of a well-known jurist.)

Valcour said: "Just as you say, Commissioner. I will keep in touch with you by radio-telephone." The commissioner was momentarily facetious: "...not even a toothbrush..." and Captain Jorgensen, looking immensely red-faced and worried, was booming: "I must have the accommodation ladder raised at once. That launch—those launches..."

"We're about to cast off, Commissioner," Valcour said.

"...Mother sill's..."

The connection broke, and Valcour, motioning to Sergeant McGuire, started along the deck. He caught in passing a glimpse of Anthony Bettle's face. It was lifted upward, staring upward (Bettle's face) like a chunk of hewn granite clouded by an intimate and special mist.

Mr. Jones, the first officer, was placidly standing by the accommodation ladder. He seemed, to Valcour, the only placid note on the entire yacht. The men in the police launches were not placid, nor were the two sailors who were standing by to raise the ladder.

"Nice night, sir," Mr. Jones said.

Valcour looked at him oddly and said: "Yes." He called over the rail to the launches and told them to shove off. He sped Sergeant McGuire down the ladder. Mr. Jones muttered a laconic command and the ladder rose alongside, and Mr. Jones, leaving such lashings as were required to the two sailors, said as he started to drift forward: "Sailing with us, sir?"

"Yes," Valcour said.

Mr. Jones's voice came casually back: "Glad of it, sir...hope you brought your gun..."

The police launches were off, gray powerful swirls in troubled oil-smooth ink, and the anchor winch clattered shrilly while from forward came the ever-excited strokes of the ship's bell—eight strokes—midnight.

Sixty seconds went by and the ship's pulse-beat was stronger as her prow with a gentle surge swung cleaving into the waters.

Where, Valcour wondered, were the people on this ship?

There was no gayety. It was not like a yachting party at all. That curious woman in the saloon, with her slashed red lips and her black eyes that were heavy and profound, with her oddly significant smile... He started walking toward the forward deck and his ears were momentarily jarred by the yacht's throbbing siren signaling an approaching craft. All alone on the empty deck, he was, until in the very bows he saw two figures standing, and one of them, as he came nearer, suddenly kneeled.

It was the woman who remained standing, with arms faint white against the flame chiffon dress, with her disturbing eyes sunk in deep shadow, and it was Anthony Bettle who was down on the deck on his knees, and Valcour stopped quite still, watching that granite face lifted with a tranquil assurance to the stars.

He heard Bettle say: "*I thank Thee and ask Thy blessing on this cause...*"

CHAPTER FOUR

FRIGHT IS GENTLE

Mrs. Anthony (Helen) Bettle gave a faint shrug and said to her brother: "Well, we're off."

Her brother, Wharton Luke, looked vague. "We have been for some time. Twenty-five years, if you wish to be exact."

Helen Bettle stood by a porthole in her cabin staring tranquilly at the sliding panorama of Manhattan's skyline. If the passing towers had exploded, one by one, she still would have stood there and watched them, quite tranquil about it. She said: "He's a good man."

Wharton's neat and compact body was tidily filling an armchair. He looked at his sister appraisingly, getting a composite, or rather a comparative, picture of her in a flash. A before-and-after picture. Helen had been slimmer and more busily pretty twenty-five years ago, with petulantly greedy little lips. She was chunkier now, and quite tranquil. Budgelessly tranquil. And the lips were smaller because they were thinner, and her eyes were baffled. Her hair clung to the period of pompadours but it was, in her case, a pompadour that had collapsed. Ratless. He said: "You ought to get a permanent."

Helen Bettle formed a faintly interested picture of her husband Anthony's reactions if she were to appear before him with her hair beautifully solidified (as she wished it were) by a permanent. She said: "They're artificial."

Wharton's smile was thin. "You could afford to buy such a good one."

Helen started to cry. Easy and noiseless tears. "I don't know." They didn't interfere (the tears) with her breathing or her talking one bit. She said again: "I don't know."

"You're an awful fool, Helen. You could have one and he'd never notice it. You think he looks at you. He doesn't."

She stopped crying and said with uncanny sureness : "Yes, he does. There isn't anything he doesn't look at." She went to a basin and wiped her eyes with a damp towel. "Anything he owns."

"I don't suppose divorce has ever occurred to you?"

"On what grounds?"

"Well, mental cruelty?"

Helen put the towel back on the rack. She said: "Don't be stupid."

"It isn't stupidity. It's stagnation."

"Then there's John."

John was her son. Hers and Anthony's. John would be twenty-one next spring, in April. A man. Helen felt there was a lot of Anthony in John. Not a replica, entirely—there was nothing tangibly solid about it, and John was more highly strung than Anthony—but the way things are in mirrors. She couldn't leave John. Nor could she (the thought almost astonished her) ever really leave Anthony. Just physical or legal distances could never separate them. Time had had the effect of attrition. There was nothing sharp-edged any more, as there had been twenty-five years ago, in her attitude toward Anthony. Just a tranquil and almost agreeable complacency. It was nice (she thought) that John did take after his father. It went for pleasantness: a frictionless and unprovocative pleasantness; and she wished that Wharton would stop his periodic efforts to stir her up. She said: "I don't want to be stirred up."

"I know you don't."

"Then why do you do it?"

"God knows. God knows why anything."

"I don't see why Anthony lets you. Why he lets you say the things you do to him."

"Every dog wants his flea."

She said querulously: "That's vulgar."

"No, it isn't. It's plain honest fact. Nothing feeds a man's sense of greatness so much as a smug attitude of indifference toward a negligible irritation. Great men have to be continually rising above things, otherwise they stop being great. Well, Anthony spends a whole lot of his time in rising above me. It's my way of paying him for food and lodging."

"That isn't fair. He thinks of you as one of the family."

"Rather as an object in his collection. I'd have a hard time getting away from him. I'm a rare piece of old pewter."

Helen looked suddenly frightened. "You aren't thinking of it, are you?"

He said: "It depends."

"Depends on what, Wharton?"

"On how all this nonsense turns out."

"Do you think it is? Do you think it's nonsense?"

"Arrant."

Helen sat down in a chair, a little heavily, and somewhat overfilling it. She said: "I wonder."

There wasn't any knock. The cabin door opened and her son, John Bettle, came in. He did look a lot like his father, she decided. Lankier, a little smaller, and younger of course. But he had her mouth. It did things (that Luke mouth) to the Bettle face. John seemed excited about something. Very pale and excited.

"The oddest thing," he said.

"What is, dear?"

"I've just heard there's a detective on board." John sat on the room's bed. "Father arranged for him to come."

Wharton said: "No guest list is complete, nowadays, without one."

John paid no attention to Wharton. He went on talking to Helen: "The wireless man told me. It has something to do, he says, with the disappearance of Mr. Hedglin. Why do you suppose he is on board, Mother?"

Helen said: "I don't know. I didn't know that Mr. Hedglin had disappeared. How did he?"

"From a taxicab."

"Surely," Wharton said, "not up in smoke?"

Helen was confused. "From a taxicab? On his way to the yacht?"

"No, after he'd left the yacht."

"But why should he leave the yacht, dear? He was sailing with us."

"I don't know."

"And if he disappeared ashore, why is a detective looking for him here?"

John said nervously: "I don't think he is." He bit a fingernail deliberately. "I think it's about somebody else."

"I don't understand, dear?"

"I think it's about Freda."

* * * *

Freda Barlowe looked at her father and said: "You're getting fat."

Horatio Barlowe glanced tolerantly down upon the copper red of his daughter's hair. "You mean I'm getting fatter. I've been fat for years." His lips smiled between plump and pleasant creases and his eyes were mechanically benevolent. Nothing applied to his evening clothes but the harried word "faultless." They did not seem to belong to him, exactly. They were too perfect for that. They were like scenery that he was using as a mask rather than as a background. Horatio Barlowe had the knowledge of correctness if not the ability to assimilate it convincingly, and nobody knew this better than himself. It was different with Freda. Her facets had the proper fires beneath them and he was sure of her;

sure that if tested she'd unquestionably cut glass. He had one of the best finishing schools for girls in the city to thank for that; the school and his own clear-headedness of foresight. He wished, tritely enough, that Ella could see her now. Ella was Freda's mother; a very simple, innocent, and lovely woman. She had died fifteen years ago, when Freda was three. "Look here," he said to Freda, "you're prettier than your mother."

Freda said: "And now what?" She smiled that odd smile of hers which always puzzled him. This, she thought, is fun. They were going to be together (she and Horatio) for the first time that she could remember; be together, that is, for any real length of time. Her affection for her father was an entirely theoretical one. It was consequently a good deal deeper than the sort which comes from long and intimate personal association. He was vague, a creature of pleasant highlights, all over reflecting surfaces.   He said: "I think we're off," and went to a porthole and drew back the curtains. His laugh was deep and soft and hearty. "Well, if Brooklyn isn't moving!"

Freda was over beside him, very close to him, very warm. You had to (he thought) get very close to a person to realize him. Body warmth was the only thing that really gave you an assurance of living. That was what was at the bottom of friendships. Not brains. Brain friendships were games. Only body warmth was living. Freda's eyes had some violet in them, the kind there is in amethysts. He thanked God she had no freckle's and that, as she had to have red hair, it had missed, by a good many degrees, being carroty. It was (he couldn't verbally place it) a swell red. She said: "We're going to get to know each other at last."   There was a moment's sudden fright in his fixedly benevolent eyes. He said: "I guess we've both been lonesome."

"Not that, so much, as incomplete."

Barlowe said a bit uncomfortably: "We're beginning to feel the swell. I never could understand yachts. I mean the mental attitude of people who buy them. Take Bettle, here—if anyone suggested he take passage for Europe on a passenger liner the size of this boat he'd think they were crazy.

Nothing would suit him but the *Bremen*. But call it a yacht!"

Freda said: "Shouldn't we go out with the others?"

He was vague about this. "I don't know."

"Why on earth not?"

He said: "No reason at all," and crossed to the door of the cabin. He held it open for Freda, who patted, as she passed him, his smooth pink cheek (*body warmth, physical contact, the humanness of it*) and said, looking at the large pearl which was a single stud in the broad expanse of his shirt: "What an oyster!"

He turned back to switch off the lights and then, standing in darkness, he heard Freda's voice in the passage saying: "I do beg your pardon! What a forcible way to meet! I'm Freda Barlowe and I weigh, as you must realize by now, a hundred and twenty pounds. I'll promise to get a pair of sea legs before the voyage is over."

And then a man's voice said: "There's nothing so surprising as the sea. I'm Valcour, a lieutenant in the detective division at headquarters."

Freda's voice said: "Really!" And Barlowe's plumpness was suddenly quite rigid, as if somebody had taken the slackness in his skin and pulled it into a knot somewhere in back of him.

"Are you heading for the saloon?" Valcour's voice said.

"With detours. I'm trailing a father behind me."

Horatio Barlowe, pleasingly, slackly plump again, stepped out into the passage and closed the cabin door.

"Here he is," Freda said. "All of him."

Barlowe's laugh was deep and soft and hearty. He said: "She imagines I'm fat. Lieutenant Valcour? I overheard the meeting."

Valcour shook the firm plump hand. "How do you do, Mr. Barlowe." He added, as the three of them started forward along the passage: "Haven't we met before?"

"Not to my knowledge, Lieutenant."

Valcour stared absently at Freda going on before them. "The world is so full of doubles," he said.

CHAPTER FIVE

A SET OF RAZORS

Burke, holding to the perpendicular with effortless ease, stepped briskly along the passage which led from the galley to the dining saloon. In his hand was a tray covered with appetizers of caviar, foie gras, and pastes. In his wake came a messboy bearing a jug of sparkling cider and a tray of glasses which had been shaped, by their designer, for the appreciative consumption of champagne.

As they swung through the dining saloon Burke said casually: "If you spill a drop of that belly-wash, I'll crack you one on the button."

The messboy, who was of Scandinavian blood but filled with an earnest desire to attain American poise and polish, said amiably: "Which button, Mr. Burke?"

Burke swayed gently for a minute and then went on. He entered the saloon in perfect balance. It was (the saloon) comfortably filled, and his eye tallied in a glance that the entire party was present. It rustled with chatter. Snatches came at him at the central table, where he was filling the champagne glasses with cider: "…so disrupting, but it doesn't matter. I've found that things only matter if you make them do so." (Mrs. Bettle, that was, tranquilly flowing even words on that stoutish Mr. Barlowe and the alertly birdlike Miss Singlestar who was, as Burke understood it, a companion for Mr. Barlowe's red-headed daughter.) "Don't you agree with me, Miss Singlestar?"

Miss Singlestar's flutelike voice came flutteringly: "Yes, but doesn't everything? Really?"

"Matter?"

"Yes. Terribly?"

Silly old ass, thought Burke, and heard Wharton Luke, over on a lounge, say to Valcour, who was sitting beside him: "Contrary to the common belief, science has really been the death of detection. It presupposes specialization, which in turn means the splitting up of an investigation into the hands of a number of men. That would be all very well if the police department could achieve perfect coordination, but is it possible? Hardly. We have strays. We have loose ends. Take, for example…"

And over there at the piano was a splash of flame chiffon, that queer Balfé woman, playing softly heaven knows what upon the keys. She was a gloomy cluck if you like, with young John Bettle hot-eyed on one side of her, draped, and young Peter Moore looking like a muscular wooden Indian standing stiff on her other side, whence he could stare at the red-headed Barlowe girl, who was talking with Mr. Bettle on a small sofa.

"Anything new," the Barlowe girl was saying, "gives me a kick."

And Horatio Barlowe, looking more granite-like and heavier than ever, answered her unsmilingly: "Nothing is new. It is only the Devil who dresses things up again freshly."

Valcour heard this, too, and said to Wharton: "Your brother-in-law takes religion seriously?"

"Anthony takes it as a reality," Wharton said. "He has been expecting to meet the Devil in person for the past three years."

Valcour's eyes were filled with flame chiffon and the muddy exoticism of the melody, or rather lack of melody, that Carlotta Balfé was playing upon the piano. He said: "And has he?"

Wharton looked at him sharply. "You're smart, Mr. Valcour."

Valcour accepted a glass of sparkling cider and a biscuit spread with caviar. "And Mr. Hedglin, has he met the Devil, too?"

Wharton refused everything. He said to Burke: "My Lithia."

Burke's face became the color of oatmeal. "It didn't come, sir."

Wharton said: "Oh."

(It wasn't, as Burke explained later to the pantryman, the word itself. "Oh" didn't mean anything. It was the way you said it. Like a nasty, thin knife, it was. The ruddy swipe!)

Wharton went on: "I am very much afraid, Mr. Valcour, that Hedglin has met something worse than the Devil. I don't like his sudden departure one bit. It's all very well for Anthony to treat it with a wave of his hand. You can't. Hedglin likes his razors."

Valcour said abruptly: "His what?"

"Hedglin has a set of razors. You know the kind: there are seven of them, one for each day in the week. If he shaved with Friday's on Monday I think he'd be physically upset."

"What about them, Mr. Luke?"

"Nothing, beyond the interesting fact that he left them behind here on the yacht."

Valcour thought about this for a moment. He said: "I see."

"I was sure that you would."

Wharton stood up. He stared with obvious distaste both at Burke and at the jug of cider, then he left the saloon by the door which opened directly onto the starboard deck.

Valcour looked thoughtfully at the closing deck door. How (he wondered) did Wharton Luke know about the set of razors having been left behind? And why? He felt a sense of acute unease. There was nothing clear-cut about the affair at all. It was a disturbing group of little intimations rather than of facts.

Waverly Hedglin was not notably an odd man. His reputation in the city was that of a substantial, clever, and highly paid consulting attorney.

The police department had no knowledge of him, in the sense of the certain suspicions or reports which were tabulated and filed concerning so many men of public, social, or of financial note. And yet Hedglin had, within the brief space of a few hours, done four odd things:

He had abruptly left the yacht without personally having spoken with either Anthony Bettle, who was his host, his client, and his friend, or with Peter Moore, his nephew and companion for the cruise.

He had left behind him on board not only his luggage but, in special, a set of razors from which he was apparently never separated. Neither of these actions had resulted from a lack of time, as he had had plenty of time in which to compose and typewrite a long and detailed note to Bettle.

He had stood on the wharf with the watchman and in spite of the coldness of the night he had taken off his hat and fanned his face.

Lastly, he had gone through that extraordinary business in the taxi-cab. Even in this there was an odd linking with the hat business on the wharf as (again in spite of the coldness) Hedglin had removed his hat and overcoat before secretly stepping out of the cab.

Peter Moore had left the piano and was coming toward him. As Peter reached the lounge, Valcour stood up and said: "You're just the man I want to see."

Peter had a strong face that just missed, for some unplaceable reason, being ugly. It was a serviceable face, plainly featured, and homely. He moved his largish, compactly muscled body with ease and slowly, and his voice was oddly gentle, as if with it (as with his impressive young strength) he did not care to break things. He said: "I was foolish to sail. I think I'll ask Mr. Bettle to put back and let me go ashore."

"Let us find some quiet place where we can talk," Valcour said.

They started for the deck door, and the music stopped on an abrupt and shocking discord. Carlotta Balfé's voice came clearly through the chatter: "You do not like my music, Peter?"

Peter looked back at her, slowly, appraisingly. "I don't think I do," he said.

CHAPTER SIX

BOWS BREAST THE OPEN SEA

It was an admirable night for that season of the year, when storms are a commonplace at sea. Ambrose Channel had been dropped astern and the lacy glitter of Coney Island was a diminishing brooch.

"People insist on associating a ship at sea with silence," Valcour said. "Especially in the nighttime. It is another example of the fallacy of legend."

There was not much wind, but the topgear was singing its thin gentle song and swinging black tracery across scattered stars while water ripped in restless surging past pressing plates.

Peter balanced by the rail, where spume flecked them saltily. "Is there any reason why I shouldn't want to go ashore, Mr. Valcour?" he said.

"Mr. Moore, you can do more for your uncle by staying aboard this yacht than by making any effort to have Mr. Bettle turn back."

"I'm afraid I don't see that."

Valcour took a cigarette case from his pocket. He offered it to Peter. "I will try and make my point clear."

"You can't smoke aboard here," Peter said. "That's another damn thing."

Valcour replaced the cigarette case. "How ever does Mr. Bettle get a crew?"

"He pays them a good deal above the average."

"Even so. There's nothing so independent as a sailor. Gold means little to them in comparison with an agreeable filling of their stomachs, and with their smokes."

Peter said carefully: "Gold means a lot to everybody, Mr. Valcour. I'll admit, though, that I've heard they're always signing on a new crew." He seemed suddenly to realize that they were leaving the important point, were being sidetracked from his determination to persuade Anthony Bettle to put the *Crusader* about and return him to port. He said: "Look here, you told me you were going to make things plain."

Valcour said abruptly: "You've lived with your uncle rather intimately, Mr. Moore?"

"Oh, for years."

"Then you can't seriously believe that he would do such an odd thing, even subconsciously?"

"As that taxicab business? Not for a minute."

"Or do you think he would have left the yacht without saying at least a word either to Mr. Bettle or to you?"

"No, I don't."

"Unless," Valcour said, "he was acting under the most extraordinary pressure."

"Pressure? Force? You mean that somebody was forcing him to leave? I don't see how. The sailor in the tender said he was quite alone."

"Certain types of force, Mr. Moore, can be exerted from a distance."

"You said you were going to be plain."

"Surely it's simple? If you had a hold over a person, some special knowledge which he didn't wish people to know about, and if you threatened to make that knowledge public unless he did certain things, tabulations show that in nine cases out of ten he would do them, even if you weren't alongside to force him physically."

"That's blackmail."

"It's a form of blackmail."

"You're accusing my uncle of having done something crooked."

"Not at all, Mr. Moore. Blackmail is equally the result of emotional folly as it is of crookedness. Everyone at some moment in his life has done at least one foolish thing. I'm simply suggesting a possible explanation for your uncle's sudden leaving of the cruise. It's the cause of his leaving that is so puzzling. We know that he did leave. Competent witnesses have told us so. What we want to know is why, and I think we can best find that out on board this yacht."

"That's all right," Peter said, "but he's ashore. There's where he needs protection. He may have gone out of his head. People do, don't they, quite suddenly?"

"Sometimes."

"Well, there you are. He may be wandering heaven knows where, and not knowing what he's doing. The whole business sounds crazy." Peter started to break away.

"One moment, Mr. Moore. Let me tell you something. The police force to the average New Yorker is a very underestimated body of men, but I can assure you of this in all seriousness. Your uncle is an important man. The commissioner has interested himself personally in this case. If, as you suggest, Mr. Hedglin should be temporarily insane he will be found within the next few hours. There isn't a man in the entire department who isn't working toward that end right now."

"Then what's to be gained by staying here?"

"Mr. Moore, I don't think your uncle is insane. I think that something has happened to him. I think the quickest way to find your uncle is first to find out what that happening was. We know it took place on this yacht. There is no possibility of your helping your uncle ashore. The department is taking better care of that than you ever could. But you may be able to help me here."

"You seem very sure."

"I have had quite a few years of experience in affairs like this."

"Of course." Peter thought for a moment. His large, muscular body was very black against the night. "I haven't meant to be rude. I'm upset. What do you suggest, Mr. Valcour? I haven't an idea what we ought to do."

"Just when did you get here? You and your uncle?"

"At nine. I'm not very used to yachts, to any kind of vessel. I know the ship's bell struck two times just as we came aboard from the tender. Uncle said that it was nine o'clock."

"What did you do, Mr. Moore?"

"Do?"

"Yes, when you both got here."

"Nothing. Nothing unusual, I mean. The steward took our bags, dropped mine off in my cabin, and then went on with Uncle to his. Look here, that's the last I saw of Uncle: just his back going down the passage after Burke."

"You stayed in your cabin?"

"Yes."

"Why?"

Peter's voice grew quicker. He said: "I'm glad you asked me that. I've just thought of something."

"Yes?"

"I stayed in my cabin, Mr. Valcour, because Uncle said he'd stop by and get me. I suppose he meant we'd meet the rest of the party together. That shows he had no intention of leaving then, doesn't it?"

"It would seem so. How long did you stay?"

"In the cabin? I pottered around, stowing my stuff away. It was more than an hour, I should think."

"Why did you leave it?"

"That girl came in. The red-headed Barlowe one." Peter was a bit stiff about this.

"Came in?"

"She mistook the cabin. She thought it was hers. I told her it wasn't and went out with her, and we found hers."

Valcour was mentally back in the passage again, with Horatio Barlowe's fluid plumpness looming before him and the nagging wonder as to where, before, he had come in contact with Barlowe's pleasantly moonlike face. He said to Peter: "You know the Barlowes?"

"No, I don't." Peter added, for no apparently good reason: "I don't like red hair."

"I thought Miss Barlowe's a sort of pleasant red; exciting, rather than ugly."

Peter said quickly: "I didn't say she was ugly. She isn't. A blind man could see that." He added belligerently: "I don't like women."

Valcour decided that Peter, at some time or other, must have been bitten. He also decided that if he was any judge of Freda's biting abilities Peter was in for being bitten again. He said: "What did you do after you succeeded in locating Miss Barlowe's cabin for her?"

"I went to Uncle's. He wasn't there, so I rooted around until I found Mr. Bettle's. He read me the note."

"Did it strike you as queer?"

"No. Mr. Bettle was very matter-of-fact about it. I just put it down to the investigation."

Valcour was interested. "What investigation, Mr. Moore?"

"The one Uncle's working on now for Mr. Bettle."

"Do you know what it's about?"

"No, but I'm sure it's important."

"From something Mr. Hedglin said?"

"From something he said about his briefcase."

"The one he took ashore with him?"

"He only had one briefcase. He said, Mr. Valcour, that it contained dynamite."

Valcour stared sharply at Peter. "Dynamite? I suppose Mr. Hedglin meant that it contained certain vital information that touched on the investigation?"

"I suppose so. He said something queer about most illusions being nothing more than delusions. He said that Mr. Bettle was going to be deeply upset."

"Come with me."

Valcour led the way to a door in the after-deck house. At his own request he had been assigned to Waverly Hedglin's cabin. He wanted to go there at once. Whatever the nature of the dynamite had been he felt that Hedglin would never have quitted the yacht without first having communicated it to Anthony Bettle. And yet Hedglin had quitted the yacht and without a word to Bettle beyond that singularly inept note, inept because of the vague unconvincingness of the excuse it contained. He said, as they went along the passage leading to his cabin: "I do not believe, Mr. Moore, that your uncle wrote that note. And if he should have written it, I don't believe that he did so willingly. Mr. Bettle has permitted me to keep it."

Valcour opened the cabin door and they went inside. He closed the door and switched on all the lights. Peter was a disturbed and heavy shadow close behind him. "I'd like to see it, the note, if you don't mind," Peter said.

"I want you to. Tell me what you think about the signature."

Valcour took the note from his pocket and handed it over to Peter, who went with it to a panel light set between opened portholes. Through them, the night was two dark disks, noisy with odd sighing sounds of wind and sea, while a noticeable roll strained the cabin with complaining creaks.

Peter looked thoughtfully at the note. He said: "I don't see anything funny about it. It seems all right to me."

"Do you get many letters from your uncle?"

"Hardly ever."

Wind was gusty through the night-black ports. "Then you're scarcely a good judge of his signature." Valcour took the note back from Peter. "I want you to be here while I go through his luggage."

"What do you expect to find?"

"I don't know."

Valcour set one of the Gladstone bags on a luggage rack. He said: "It isn't locked. Does he keep his bags unlocked?"

"No, he always locks them."

"I see." Valcour opened the bag. Its contents were stuffed confusion. "This bag has been gone through already, Mr. Moore." In his mind was a picture of Wharton Luke, spurning cider, and remarking so casually that Hedglin had gone ashore without taking with him his set of razors.

Peter was staring down into the bag. "This is getting serious," he said.

"It always has been."

"Can't something be done?"

"Quite a few things are being done. You needn't worry about the city end of it."

The contents of the bag were the ordinary lot of things a man would carry on a cruise. Everything was conservatively plain and of good material. The second Gladstone bag was in a similar state of messed confusion, and held nothing of interest. In the wardrobe suitcase, Valcour found a leather writing case.

The writing case interested him because it was empty. He wondered whether in it the person who had gone so messily and hastily through the luggage had found what he had wanted. They would be papers of some nature, but scarcely of importance, or else why hadn't Hedglin carried them off with him in that dynamite-containing briefcase? He replaced the writing case and closed the suitcase. He opened a portable typewriter that was standing on a desk, took the magnifying lens from his pocket, and examined the keys.

"Fingerprints?" Peter said. The lens impressed him.

"That's the trouble. There aren't any. The keys have been wiped off." He pressed a button set in the paneling, in the hope that it would produce the steward.

"The note was a forgery?"

"Your uncle would scarcely have wiped off the keys, Mr. Moore. I don't understand this situation at all. There is only one sane solution."

"Yes?"

"Your uncle is still on board the yacht."

CHAPTER SEVEN

WIND WHIPS DARK SILK

Peter said: "That's crazy."

"Yes. Quite crazy."

"Then why say it's a sane solution? Several people saw my uncle leave the yacht."

"That's why it's crazy."

"It isn't a matter for joking about."

Valcour was courteously serious. "I don't make a practice of joking about things, Mr. Moore." Burke rapped on the door, opened it, and said: "You rang, sir?"

Valcour nodded toward the rack above the basin. "Who changes the water in that carafe, steward?"

"I do, sir."

"When did you fill it last?"

"Around six o'clock this evening."

"Would any of your men have touched it since then?"

"Not likely, Mr. Valcour. It's quite full. It hasn't been used."

"You use bottled water in the carafes?"

"Oh, yes, sir."

"Take a look at the water that's in it now, please."

Burke went over and picked up the carafe. He held it against a light. "It's a bit muggy." He tasted a drop or two and spat in the basin. "From the taps. It's very peculiar, if I may say so. I don't understand it, I really don't." He looked suddenly frightened. "I do hope to God that Mr. Luke's—"

"I don't think you need worry about Mr. Luke's carafe, Burke."

"I do most earnestly hope so, sir. I think I'd have to leave, I would."

"Was it you who delivered that note which Mr. Hedglin left for Mr. Bettle?"

"Yes."

"Did Mr. Hedglin say anything to you, anything odd, when he gave it to you?"

"He didn't give it to me, Mr. Valcour."

"You weren't on hand when he left?"

"No. I didn't see Mr. Hedglin again after I racked his stuff here in the cabin."

"Who did give you the note?"

"Hanson. He's the sailor who ran the tender while we were in port. Mr. Hedglin gave it to him when they reached the dock to carry back to me. Mr. Hedglin had forgot about it."

Peter said: "My uncle doesn't forget things like that."

Burke was defensive. "Maybe in the hurry, Mr. Moore?"

"I'd like to see Hanson at once. Can you get him for me?"

"Yes, Mr. Valcour."

Burke started for the door, and then hesitated.

Valcour said: "Well?"

"That carafe, I'll just change the water."

"Leave it as it is, please."

"But you can't drink the taps, sir."

"I don't want to drink it. Is there a safe on board?"

"Mr. Bettle has one, and so has the captain."

"Can you get me some rubber?"

"Rubber?"

"Yes."

Burke said it again: "Rubber?"

"Canvas will do if you haven't any rubber. I want to cap the top of that carafe before it's put in the captain's safe."

Burke said: "Very good, sir." He thought: Nuts. He left.

"I don't see what you're driving at," Peter said.

Valcour was nervous. Wind through an open port was damp and cold on his cheek. "I can't picture your uncle emptying that carafe and then refilling it with tap water. Can you?"

"No."

"Even," Valcour added almost to himself, "if he had first spilled a lot of it on the center of this rug."

"Why do you say that?"

"These spots. They're still damp, if you care to feel them. He might have dropped the carafe, but why refill it with tap water and then wipe it clear of fingerprints?"

"You do see a lot of odd things," Peter said. "The carafe is important enough to lock up in a safe?"

Valcour was vague. "If it should turn out that something has happened to your uncle, I've a feeling that the carafe will be quite important."

Peter said suddenly: "See here, I wonder if we're overemphasizing?"

"You can't overemphasize the fantastic."

"Fantastic?"

"That's what this case is. Bizarre, if you prefer the word. I wish you knew the nature of the investigation that your uncle is making, or that Mr. Bettle would tell me."

"You've asked him?"

"Yes. He said it couldn't be pertinent." Valcour was almost irritable. "Secrecy is a vice with rich men. They nurture it as a form of self-protection." He said suddenly: "Mr. Moore, why did you continue on with the trip?"

"After I knew Uncle wasn't coming?"

"Yes."

Peter looked uncomfortable. He said: "It would have disappointed me not to. Mr. Bettle insisted there was no reason why I shouldn't. As I've said, I've never been on a yacht. I haven't gone many places. I guess everyone wants to go places."

Valcour was careful. "You are dependent on your uncle?"

The flush on Peter's cheek deepened. "Quite dependent."

There was a knock on the door, and Valcour said: "Come in."

Burke came in, followed by Hanson. Hanson was young, candidly vague as to eye, and almost equally so as to teeth. He was very scrubbed, and redly bronzed by wind and sun.

"Here's Hanson," Burke said. "And here is a rubber bathing cap. Perhaps it might do?"

"It will do very well. Thank you, Steward." Valcour stared at Hanson, at his serene and not unlikable dumbness. He indicated Peter. "You brought this man and another man from the wharf to the yacht this evening?"

"Yes, sir."

"What did the man who came with this one look like?"

Hanson turned calm and friendly eyes to the ceiling in search of some inspirational message. "Like anyone, sir."

"Would you recognize him again?"

This was a lot easier. "I did. I recognized him when I took him back to the dock." Hanson clinched the point: "He looked just the same."

"And how was that?"

"Same gray hair, same muffler, same coat and same hat."

Valcour felt that he knew the answer even before he asked the question. "How do you know his hair was gray?"

"He took off his hat."

It was there again: this odd insistence on the part of Hedglin of taking off his hat in unlikely places. "Was the wind blowing strongly?"

"No, sir. There wasn't no wind, not then."

"How did you know his hair was gray the first time, when you brought him and Mr. Moore out to the yacht?"

"His hat fell off when he got into the tender. I handed it to him and he put it back on again."

Peter said: "That's right. I remember that."

Valcour asked Hanson: "Do you remember how he wore the muffler?"

"Yes, sir. Around his neck."

"I mean did he wear it plainly? Well up, so that you could see it plainly?"

"Oh, yes, sir. It almost covered his chin."

"He gave you a note when you brought him back to the wharf. What did he say when he handed it to you?"

"He said he'd forgotten about it. I was to take it right back to the yacht and see it was delivered to Mr. Bettle."

"Did his voice sound nervous?"

"No."

"Did he himself seem nervous?"

"No, sir."

"Did he talk with you at all on the way to the wharf?"

"No, sir. I passed a remark or two about the weather. It was good weather. He just made noises."

"Noises?"

"He made noises like grunts. He didn't seem interested in the weather."

"Thank you."

"Sir?"

"Thank you, that is all."

"Yes, sir."

Hanson left the cabin, and Burke said: "I brought some twine, too, Mr. Valcour. For the carafe."

Valcour took the rubber bathing cap and string. He fastened securely the top of the carafe. Burke, who wanted to be quite sure, as well as to give a last-minute benefit of the doubt, said: "It's to go in the captain's safe?"

"Yes."

"He'll never know what to make out of it."

"I'll explain."

"He's a man, if I may say so, who is easily upset. He has his peevish moments. Like the best of us. Shall I take it up to him, sir?"

"I'll take it."

Burke was relieved. "Very good, Mr. Valcour."

"Do you happen to know where I'll find Miss Carlotta Balfé?"

"I just passed her on deck, sir."

"Thank you." The capped carafe was loosely held in his hand. "If you gentlemen will pardon me, I am going out on deck."

Peter said: "You shan't want me with you?"

"Not just at present, Mr. Moore."

Valcour waited until Peter and Burke had left the cabin, then he went out into the passage and locked the cabin door. He made his way to the deck and at its stern, by the taffrail, he found Carlotta Balfé. A wrap of dark silk was flimsy about her, and wind whipped it sharply.

Carlotta said, as Valcour stopped beside her: "You, too, think he is dead."

CHAPTER EIGHT

DEAD MEN STARE

It astonished Valcour to realize that he did. He thought exactly that: *Hedglin is dead*. There was no sense to it, and certainly no sane foundation in fact. He looked at Carlotta Balfé steadily, while night-softened harshnesses in her face and her eyes stared calmly back from thick and impressive shadows. They were open very wide, her eyes. They were asleep. He said: "You are psychic?"

Her smile came slowly. "We are both of us psychic. You have come to ask me, Mr. Valcour, about my last view of Waverly Hedglin."

His own smile was disarming. "Among several things."

Carlotta said carefully: "What sort of things, Mr. Valcour?"

Her eyes, he knew, had immediately observed the carafe. They kept returning to it. Drawn to it. He wondered just when she would refer to it. He said: "Where were you when you saw Mr. Hedglin leave the yacht, Miss Balfé?"

"Shall I show you?"

"If you please."

Her fingers rested on his arm, and wind slashed the dark silk of her wrap extravagantly as they walked to a chair near the starboard side of the after-deck.

"You can see the accommodation ladder from here," she said.

"You were sitting here?"

"Yes"

"Alone?"

"Alone."

"Was that awning light by the head of the ladder turned on?"

"Yes. I could see Mr. Hedglin quite clearly."

Valcour asked, almost with resignation: "With his hat on?"

Carlotta seemed surprised at that. "Why, yes. He would scarcely have had it off, would he?"   Valcour's smile was brief. "Are you familiar enough with Mr. Hedglin to know his mannerisms?"

"I don't think I understand."

Valcour wondered at Carlotta's nervous lightness. Her manner had the glitter of bright glass globes. "I mean," he said, "are you familiar with his carriage, with the way he walks, with the little movements which a person makes that stamp him individually."

"I'm afraid I am not." She added earnestly: "But I am sure it was he—I can see what you are driving at—I am sure it was he."

"Then why do you feel he is dead?"

This recurrence to her original idea seemed to shock her. She said: "Did I?" She went on with stupid haste: "I did. Of course I did. I still do."

"But why?"

"You are not aware of my calling, Mr. Valcour?"

The term was confusing. "Your profession, your vocation, Miss Balfé? I'm not."

She said hurriedly: "My name is gradually becoming identified with psychic investigation. I've never sought publicity. I am not in it for money. Such gifts as mine—" Such gifts, her shrug implied, were beyond the reach of any monetary compensation.

He said: "That is interesting," and "I see." It explained several things, possibly, including that bizarre tableau at the moment of the yacht's sailing when Carlotta had been a streak of flame chiffon in the bows, and Anthony Bettle a statue done in granite kneeling on the deck.

Carlotta said: "It came to me about twenty-four minutes after ten."

"The impression that Mr. Hedglin was dead?" She corrected him gently. "The knowledge."

"Then as Mr. Hedglin left the yacht at about half-past nine, he was killed in the city?"

Her breath came sharply, and she said: "I didn't say killed. I said he was dead." Her fingers were painfully tight about his wrist. "What have you found out? What do you know?"

His answer was consciously vague. "Need we eliminate the possibility of an accident? Mr. Hedglin's actions were erratic. The traffic of New York is not a thing to be erratic in."

She came to it at last, with startling abruptness, and said: "Mr. Valcour, will you tell me why you are carrying that carafe?"

"Because it is filled with tap water."

Carlotta's skin was no longer pale. It was pallid. She said: "Not salt?"

"Salt water? From the sea?"

Her effort to regain control over herself was noticeable. "I am being stupid."

Carlotta refused to go on with her odd reaction as to the water in the carafe being neither bottled nor tap water, but salt. She clung to indecisiveness, to impulsive ejaculations that were meaningless. There was a growing coldness about her, and she held the flimsy wrap more tightly, as a sheath, while Valcour wondered whether she were being professionally remote.

He changed the subject. "Did Mr. Hedglin say anything to you on his way to the ladder, Miss Balfé?"

"He didn't pass me. He came out by that door and went directly to the ladder. I called, but he didn't answer."

"He struck you as being nervous?"

Carlotta thought about this impartially. "No, not nervous, Mr. Valcour. Preoccupied."

Burke was drifting down upon them, leaning back against a propelling wind. He said to Valcour: "I beg your pardon. I shouldn't interrupt, I'm sure, but you're wanted on the telephone."

It was still reasonably new, this magical feat of talking with a person who was ashore from the sea, and Valcour was mildly thrilled about it. He said: "Thank you, Steward. You will excuse me, Miss Balfé?"

Carlotta said hurriedly: "We will talk again, Mr. Valcour?"

"We will talk again."

"The wireless room is this way, sir."

"Thank you."

It was the commissioner's voice that reached Valcour when he lifted the receiver to his ear.

"Valcour?" the commissioner said. "Anything at your end?"

"Several things, Commissioner."

"We've a blank here. We've worried the life out of the taxi driver, and there's only one point: the right-hand door of his cab sticks. That's why Hedglin got out on the left and the traffic man was able to see him. It also shows that Hedglin wasn't acting subconsciously, or he'd have used the right-hand door. He deliberately wanted to get out of that cab without letting the driver know it. You can see what details we're reduced to. The press is onto the business, by the way. What are your leads?"

Valcour glanced around the wireless room. The operator, trying most obviously not to listen, was drinking in each word. Burke hovered purposelessly by the deck door. "Nothing, Commissioner."

"I see. You can't talk privately, is that it?"

"Yes, that's it."

"There is nothing you can tell me that will help us immediately?"

"Nothing."

"They have ordinary wireless on board, of course?"

"Yes, Commissioner."

"Then if anything comes up that needs immediate attention you'd better communicate by code. I realize you are on the track of something."

"There's something."

"You'll radio at once as soon as it breaks?"

"At once."

"This is most unsatisfactory. You must try to arrange for privacy. Telephony is so much quicker."

"I will. It isn't essential right now. There's nothing immediate."

"I realize that. Well, I'll be right here. As it looks just now, I'll be here all night." The commissioner became momentarily personal. "Everything all right? Comfortable?"

"Yes. The steward fixed me up with essentials."

"That's good. Good-night."

"Good-night, Commissioner."

Valcour hung up, and Anthony Bettle was suddenly in the wireless room, filling it hugely, very overpowering with his stonelike shagginess. "You've just been talking with the commissioner?" he said. "Is there any news?"

"None, Mr. Bettle."

Bettle shepherded Valcour outside and down the ladder to the main deck. "That's good, isn't it? I mean in the sense that no news is good news. There's more truth than people give them credit for in the old saws."

Valcour said: "I wish that you would tell me, Mr. Bettle, the nature of the inquiry Mr. Hedglin is making for you."

Bettle stopped by the rail and stared across the windy pitch-black sea. His voice, when he spoke, was final. "There can be no connection, Mr. Valcour. Later, if eventualities make me feel that the matter might be pertinent—Eventualities? We are talking like schoolboys. What eventualities could there possibly be?"

His face was quite close to Valcour's, his voice raised to carry above the ripping slap of water and the whipping wind.

Valcour said steadily: "Carlotta Balfé believes that Mr. Hedglin is dead."

The change was terrific. It was as shocking as granite melting beneath some special heat. Bettle didn't speak for a moment. He couldn't speak. At last he said: "She said that?"

"She believes that he died at twenty-four minutes after ten."

All of his strength seemed to have gone from Bettle. The vigor which had contradicted his years had become flaccid. There was a brokenness about him. He turned, and his step on the deck was shambling, and Valcour heard him say: "Then may God have mercy on his soul."

* * * *

Miss Singlestar stared at the traveling clock that stood on a dresser in her cabin. It pointed to two o'clock. She marked her place in a novel she was reading, closed the book, and put it on a table beside her chair. She didn't feel tired. Not a bit. She sat there drinking it in: the impossible pleasure of being in her own cabin on board a yacht. Going places.

The Ragged Island of Jumentos Cays (the names were romantic music singing with unaccustomed melody inside of her little old head) *which one reached through the Hole-in-the-Wall which lay between Great Abaco and Kleuthera Islands of the Bahama group and then along the Tongue-of-Ocean past the Isles of Andros...*

This first night.

Nothing, she realized, would ever again equal the pleasant happiness of this first night. She didn't want to give it up. She wanted to keep sitting there, feeling the novel and (fortunately for her) fascinating motion of the yacht. She thought of it as majestic. There was something majestic about it: the steady, surging rise (like a dart, like a rich and expensive arrow darting through air), then the slight, protesting shudder, the settling, and the impressive rising all over again. She also wanted to go to bed.

In that satined bed.

In spite of, or even because of, its almost vulgar air of richness, she wanted to get into that satin-covered bed. But if she did, she'd go to sleep, and then it would be all over—this exquisite first moment, this happy night which she was hugging so intimately, to be stored for later, less satined days, when the only light left would be memories.

A turn on deck. That was it...

The wind and shock of the sea against plates surprised her. She wasn't frightened. She felt oddly exhilarated, and after an experimental step or two managed to keep her footing fairly steadily. Brine stung minutely against her cheeks and she accepted it eagerly, pressing her silly little face right into the wind, blinking her eyes.

She almost had stumbled over the large basket chair on the after-deck before she realized that a man was sitting in it. She said: "I *do* beg your pardon." She added happily: "My eyes are full of salt."

The man didn't say anything. Her stumble had brought Miss Single-star's face quite close to his. Shock drained the color from it, and she said: "Mr. *Hedglin!*—Forgive my being startled—we—I understood you had gone ashore."

She stood there stupidly clutching the back of the basket chair. She wished that Mr. Hedglin would say something, instead of just sitting and staring.

Staring.

She said: "I'll be going. I'm sorry if I disturbed you."

Her voice sounded foolish. The yacht gave a deeper roll and the man's hand, which had been resting on the arm of the basket chair, slipped off and slid slowly along the chair's side. Like a sleeper's. But his eyes were open. With that dreadful staring. With (she knew it suddenly, surely) that dreadful, final staring of the dead.

PART TWO

CHAPTER NINE

BLOOD SHOWS IN MOONLIGHT

Captain Jorgensen stared at moonbeams patterning and drifting on the ceiling above his bunk. Four bells sounded from the near-by bridge. Two o'clock. His eyes were wide open, staring up at the shifting pattern of the moonbeams. He reviewed several things.

What he had eaten.

It must have been something he had eaten that had caused this unnatural and wasteful wakefulness during the hours which were allotted from the day for refreshing sleep.

A carafe with a cerise rubber bathing cap tied about its neck. In his safe.

He purpled a little even at this hundredth recollection of the fact. What, pray, was the sea coming to? Mysteries. His snort at mysteries, chiefly involving cerise-capped carafed ones, lifted his head a good inch from the pillow. And no explanation about it. Mild as you please he had been (Valcour) with his: "If you will be so kind, Captain." And his oddly earnest insistence that no one was to remove the carafe but himself.

Vague. All vague. And here it was four bells, and where was sleep? He envied the first officer, Mr. Jones, so busily mooning on the bridge, facing the refreshing salt breeze, amused by the moon and her companionable stars, being, in fact, properly awake whereas he (the captain) should be, and wasn't, properly asleep.

The excited rapping on his door came as an agreeable shock.

Something (thank God) had happened. Nothing serious, nothing catastrophic (the *Crusader* herself was pursuing with businesslike smoothness her swift sharp way), but something that would prove an excuse for this wretched and wasteful wakefulness.

He called "Come in!" and switched on a bed light. He incidentally made a grab for the covers while his eyes stared in China-blue astonishment above a blanket's rim at Miss Singlestar. At, he thought, as soon as he could think anything, a ghost of Miss Singlestar. "My dear lady," he said, "what has happened? What is the meaning of this?"

He swiftly reviewed possibilities: sleep-walking? She did look dazed. Calling? Certainly not. Not calling. He was considering illness, or imaginary fears (how frightened she looked—he noticed it now), when she said: "He is in a chair on the back deck. He is dead."

It was several minutes later before Captain Jorgensen realized that his striped pajamas were on view from his central position on the floor of the cabin. "Nonsense," he said soothingly. Then he said it more sharply: "Nonsense!" Dead people in chairs were an impossibility on the after-decks of yachts.

Miss Singlestar's voice was white, as her face was white, and all pinched. "It is Mr. Waverly Hedglin, Captain. He is dead."

This was perfectly obvious madness. Waverly Hedglin was ashore. That was what all the fuss at sailing time had been about: the absolute and ascertained fact that Waverly Hedglin was ashore. It was why Valcour was aboard, although why Valcour should be aboard when the disappearing Hedglin was ashore was more than Captain Jorgensen could see. It was why (he realized his pajamas) that cerisely rubber-stopped carafe was in his safe. "You must excuse me." He clutched a toweling bathrobe which, when struggled into, covered his bigness sketchily. "You are dreaming, Miss Singlestar, or else somebody is playing, for you, a distasteful joke." He said loudly: "Mr. Hedglin is ashore."

Her gentleness was terrifying. "He is sitting in a chair on the back deck. Dead."

There was a disturbing convincingness about it: the gentle reiteration of Waverly Hedglin's deadness. He snatched a flashlight and said: "Come!"

He led the way, his bathrobe a pennant in the strong chill breeze, with Miss Singlestar as a fragile tender in his burly wake. They reached the after-deck and stared at empty chairs.

She said: "That was the chair."

Dreams. The mad stuff that makes up dreams. He grew coldly, loudly polite. "Emptiness. In that chair, dear lady, sits emptiness. Go back to bed and in the morning this distressing nightmare will be forgotten."

"I haven't been to bed, Captain." (How cold the wind was, how merciless the indifferent sea, how bitter was the sweet fruit of romance when it is turned, by death, to puckering ashes!)

"You haven't been to bed?" Could one dream such nonsense when awake? No. "You must go back to it at once."

He was getting quite upset, and was aware once again of the inadequacies of his toilet. He would probably have done something active about getting her back into her denied bed again had she not, just then, said: "Where the moon strikes the back of the chair." Like a run-down phonograph record, her voice was.

He said: "Yes? I do not see a thing."

"It glistens, don't you think? That little spot?" It did. It glistened. Little and globular and black. It was a blackness that became, under the shaft of the electric torch, a dark and nasty-looking red. Shock erased Captain Jorgensen's irritability. Blood was concrete evidence of definite things, even of death. He was a thoroughly alarmed and worried man. He was also an immediately efficient one, now that he had something tangible to cling to in this wicked-looking dull-sheened drop. He said: "I must go to the bridge and have our headway cut down. We will zigzag back over our course. Tell me quickly, dear lady, what happened here?"

Miss Singlestar felt sick. Very sick. And Captain Jorgensen was a loud voice coming at her from idiotically swirling striped linen and meager toweling. It was so foolish for that voice to say that they would zigzag back over their course, as if Mr. Hedglin had gone overboard. She said: "He couldn't have gone overboard, because he was dead."

"Yes, yes,"—that loud, that pounding voice—"but what happened? What did you see?"

Her legs were so wretchedly strengthless, as if they'd been running for blocks and blocks (as they sometimes did in her dreams after a tiring day) in chase of a slowly moving streetcar. She was sinking easily, and as a balloon must sink, into a chair. "Nothing happened." How inefficient her own voice was against that booming one! "I came out to walk on deck. To make it last a little longer."

"Make *what* last longer, dear lady?"

Miss Singlestar felt she couldn't possibly explain that. Not now. She ignored it utterly and said: "I suppose I wasn't noticing just where I was going. There was salt in my eyes and I almost stumbled into a chair." How cold the night seemed when you were sick with horror! She attempted to rise with her useless legs. "Into this chair—"

Captain Jorgensen was not effective at faintings. He shouted at the very top of his capable lungs: "Stewardess!" And Carlotta, dripping dark silk, was running toward him lightly. She said: "She is ill?"

"She has fainted. There is the very devil to pay." There were ten thousand things to do at once. A man who by rights should have disappeared in New York and have stayed disappeared was now on board. Worse. He was not on board. He was drifting somewhere astern. A fainted woman. Another who might well join her swiftly in fainting. That would make two fainted women. His face pressed redly close to Carlotta's and he said: "Do not you faint until the stewardess comes. This little lady, you will fix her. You will please douse her with water. The stewardess, I have called her, she will douse with you."

Carlotta stared speculatively after Captain Jorgensen's hurrying bulk. She waited patiently until his striped-linen legs had vanished up the ladder to the boat deck. She took a handkerchief that was in her hand and leaned over Miss Singlestar, who was slumped forward in the wicker chair. Carlotta said softly: "Miss Singlestar! Miss Singlestar!" and shook her by the shoulders.

The shaking slumped Miss Singlestar against the back of the chair. Carlotta straightened up and walked a deliberate step or two toward the rail.

"I wonder," said Valcour who appeared (as it seemed to Carlotta) out of dark nowhere. "whether you could tell me why Captain Jorgensen called for the stewardess, and what has happened here."

Carlotta said: "You startled me." She looked at his clothing. "You are still up."

"We are still up." He stressed the pronoun slightly.

Carlotta hesitated for a moment. She said: "The night is my province."

"Miss Singlestar has been taken ill?"

"She has fainted."

"Why?"

"I don't know."

"Captain Jorgensen said nothing?"

"He said that she had fainted."

"Where did he hurry to just now?"

"To get the stewardess." Carlotta stepped a little closer to the rail.

"We're slowing down. We're losing headway. Why?"

"Odd." Her voice was completely controlled. "It's very odd."

He started to close in on her, and something small and square and white dropped lazily from the rail and settled on the water.

"Your handkerchief, Miss Balfé."

Carlotta looked indifferently down at the little square drifting astern. "Careless of me, Mr. Valcour. No matter."

"Beautifully careless," he said.

CHAPTER TEN

THE SPOT MARKED "X"

It was there again, that faint and puzzling smile, which Valcour had first noticed when he had passed through the saloon with Bettle just before sailing time.

Carlotta said: "That is a peculiar choice of an adverb, Mr. Valcour."

Valcour was holding Miss Singlestar forward, flashing a small electric torch over the wicker of the chair, over the back of Miss Singlestar's dress. "Naturally you would not care to keep the handkerchief, Miss Balfé, if it were stained with blood."

"Blood?" Carlotta was beside him, very near, staring sharply at the chair. "Is there blood?"

"Fortunately the chair is wicker."

"But I don't understand?"

"There are interstices in wicker." Valcour was kneeling on the deck in front of Miss Singlestar, looking up at her.

Carlotta said: "We must do something for her. Where is the stewardess? Captain Jorgensen went to get the stewardess."

"The yacht has stopped."

"It is dangerous to leave a person in a faint. She ought to lie down. We ought to put her on a couch or some place."

"Miss Singlestar has come to. The yacht has stopped."

"Come to?"

"Her eyes are opening. Her pulse is normal."

"Then she will tell us what made her ill."

"She will tell us, Miss Balfé, what shocked her. The yacht is turning back upon our course."

The *Crusader* came about and a searchlight was brilliant from the bridge, shafting slowly back and forth across the waters, making sullen ink of valleys with glittering white frothing crests. Valcour stood up and looked steadily at Carlotta, at her smudgy eyes centered with buttons of smooth jet. He thought: *If I could get her to talk, this case would be solved to-night*. Footsteps were sounding sharply along the deck as Anthony Bettle and Captain Jorgensen came toward them.

Bettle was saying: "…this unnecessary delay."

"Again I must tell you," Captain Jorgensen was answering loudly, "that as a seaman it is my duty to turn back and search for the body."

"But why not search the yacht first? If there is a body."

"That is being done. The steward is making the search now."

They were close to the wicker chair and Bettle, with a singularly disinterested voice, said: "Show me the blood." He ignored Carlotta and Miss Singlestar, not with any deliberate rudeness but as if (as it was) his mind were thoroughly preoccupied with compelling and private affairs. His eyes rested on Valcour, went through him…

Valcour said: "The blood spot is no longer there, Mr. Bettle."

"Oh? Ah, yes, Mr. Valcour. But it was there? You did see it?"

"No, but I would like your permission to cut a small square of wicker from this chair back."

Bettle was completely indifferent. "If you wish," he said.

"I repeat that I saw it—Hah! the little lady is coming to." Captain Jorgensen bent solicitously over Miss Singlestar. He raised his powerful voice to shake from her the last vestiges of her faint. "You will explain, please, that it was you who discovered the blood?"

The word almost sickened her again, and Miss Singlestar placed her hand on Captain Jorgensen's muscular arm. "I would like to get out of this chair," she said.

"Of course! There, that is better. Now you will tell us what it was you saw."

The voice was mallet blows, but the arm was steadying her most comfortingly and the stewardess, a raw-boned, disillusioned-looking woman with a cap that hinted at a concealed bun, had come along the deck and was on the other side of her. Miss Singlestar said: "I am quite all right now, really. I'm sorry to have caused such bother." Not for years had she been bothered about. Always it had been the other way, with herself doing the bothering-about for other people's comforts. It was remarkably pleasant. This solicitude.

Valcour said gently: "What was it that startled you, Miss Singlestar? You came upon someone who was dead?"

"I came out for a turn on deck, Mr. Valcour. You see, I wanted to make it last…" How automatically the words were coming and falling into their familiar sentences!

They listened to her until she was quite through, then Valcour said: "Did you notice any wound, Miss Singlestar?"

"No, Mr. Valcour." She was determined not to faint again. (How intent that odd Miss Balfé seemed.) "I saw no wound. Mr. Hedglin's face was very peaceful, as if he had passed away in his sleep. Quite quiet and peaceful."

Bettle's voice was querulous. "This whole business is incomprehensible. We know that Hedglin went ashore before we sailed." He said deliberately to Miss Singlestar: "You came upon some man seated in this chair. Your stumbling over it woke him up. He may have been dazed with sleep. Some people are dazed when they're wakened suddenly. That's all there was to it: he sat there dazed. Your imagination did the rest. You left, and then he got up and went away."

"What man got up and went away, Mr. Bettle?" Valcour said.

Bettle was vague again, sinking securely back into the inner racings of his busy mind. "Possibly one of us, Mr. Valcour. Perhaps some member of the crew." His manner said: *Now that I have solved this business, I wish that you would not annoy me with stupid and irritating trifles.*

Captain Jorgensen was shocked. "A seaman sitting on the afterdeck? Impossible!"

"Oh, but it wasn't a seaman. I am sure it was Mr. Hedglin." Miss Singlestar was insistent. "I have seen Mr. Hedglin before, you know."

Bettle said: "There is no light by this chair." His gaze at Miss Singlestar was something in the nature of the sort one turns on a gnat.

"But as I've told you, Mr. Bettle, I stumbled and my face was quite close to his." (How tiresomely difficult some people could be when faced with the obvious! It was almost as if Mr. Bettle were purposefully, stubbornly refusing to admit facts that were, to her, so absolute.) "It was very gray, his face. I recognized him clearly. His eyes weren't open the way a person's are when he wakes up suddenly. There was no life in them. It is hard to explain, but he was dead."

Burke, a little breathless, and followed more leisurely by Wharton Luke, joined them hurriedly. He said to Captain Jorgensen: "I've checked up on everybody, sir. They're all accounted for. Everybody is on board." He added as an afterthought: "And nobody's dead."

Wharton was spectacular in colored silk. The dressing gown fitted him snugly, and his dark hair was carefully brushed. "Where," he said amiably, "shall I find the hallucinations?"

"It *ain't* hallucinations, sir," Burke said. "As I've taken the liberty to explain to you a thousand times, it's a missing corpse."

Wharton eyed Burke coldly. "Lithia!" He turned to Valcour: "Am I to understand, my dear Valcour, that one of us died, fell overboard, and still we're all here? The problem, if it were not so late at night, would be enchanting."

Bettle showed some signs of interest. "Wharton," he said, "that's the first sensible remark I've heard you make since I've known you."

"You must accept my apologies, Anthony."

Valcour said to Burke: "You have spoken with everybody?"

Burke, who fancied himself as somewhat of a *littérateur*, said: "To the last man, sir."

"If you will forgive me—I think my room—" Miss Singlestar's voice was faint. "Of course if I could be of any further assistance—"

Mrs. Wiggins, the stewardess, stared at the men inclusively. Her disillusioned-looking eyes were prominent and fishlike. "It's about time," she said.

She started to lead Miss Singlestar away (to find cold comfort for the rest of the night beneath that satin spread), and Carlotta moved as if to go with them.

Bettle interrupted Carlotta and said: "Carlotta, what about this?" He looked at her almost plaintively, and added: "Hadn't we better?"

She seemed suddenly tired. Drained-looking. "It is rather late, Anthony. But if you think…perhaps it would be best."

She placed a hand on Bettle's arm. They became at once intimately, completely absorbed in one another. Miss Singlestar and Mrs. Wiggins had gone, and their own steps died out along the silent deck while Valcour, Burke, Captain Jorgensen, and Wharton Luke stared at an empty wicker chair.

"The spot marked 'X,' Mr. Valcour?"

"Yes, Mr. Luke. That is the spot marked 'X.'"

CHAPTER ELEVEN

SQUIRREL-CAGE BLUES

Six bells, with their important, brittle syncopation, came faintly from forward to the wicker chair, and Wharton said: "The unearthly hour that people will pick out for crimes! Three o'clock. They always are fondly deluded with the impression that the rest of the world will be tightly asleep. It never is. There is either the old gentleman with sciatica or the woman with toothache. In this instance, there's us. I am constitutionally unfitted for saying 'we.' Should I have, or not?"

In spite of the chill temperature Captain Jorgensen was gradually heating up. Wharton's voice wasn't bothering him, or the things Wharton was saying. He didn't hear the things Wharton was saying. He wasn't listening. He was watching, slightly pop-eyed, while Valcour sliced a square of wicker with a pocket knife from the back of the remarkable chair; remarkable in that people who sat in it were either dead or not, or in it or out. He was hotly aware of Valcour's request even before Valcour made it.

"I must ask you, Captain," Valcour said, "to keep this small square of wicker in your safe with the carafe."

Wharton was charmed. He said: "Exhibit 'B'?"

Valcour smiled back pleasantly. "I should call it, rather, the corpus delicti."

"That is interesting, my dear Valcour. I am not very versed in the laws of criminal evidence. There has been, as yet, no pertinent occasion to become so."

(*It isn't even wicker*, thought Captain Jorgensen, mulling. *It's a corpus delicti.*)

"You see, Mr. Luke, if a proper chemical or microscopic examination should show that there is human blood in the fibers or in the space between the basket weave, it will go to substantiate Miss Singlestar's evidence that there was a dead man in the chair."

"In other words, a circumstantial corpse."

"Exactly."

Wharton said: "This is perfectly delightful, and I don't mind being out of bed a bit. The corpse, of course, need not necessarily have been Waverly Hedglin's?"

Valcour was careful. "If Mr. Hedglin is picked up in New York it will disprove that the body in the chair was his."

"No hog, my dear Valcour, could go in for better hedging. Or is it too early for puns? I don't think it is. And why are you so certain that it was a body? Why not, as my astute brother-in-law pointed out, a man who simply got up and walked away?"

"Because of the strong resemblance to Mr. Hedglin. It was obviously the criminal's purpose to establish the fact that Mr. Hedglin was ashore and did not sail with the yacht. For the criminal then to go ahead and establish him aboard the yacht would be an absurdity touching on lunacy."

"If you will be so good as to give me that bit of wicker, Mr. Valcour, I will put it in my safe and return to the bridge." Captain Jorgensen knew when he was hot enough. Yachts! Carafes, and delicted corpses, and windy measured words. He wanted to get busy and have the ship searched at once, so that if there *was* a plain-labeled corpse on board he could produce it. They (corpses) were very bad for ships. "I am going to have the ship searched. I also wish to observe our position. I believe we have about reached the spot where Miss Singlestar became aware of the doings in this chair. If so we will discontinue further fruitless zigzagging and put back upon our course."

"Thank you, Captain."

Captain Jorgensen accepted the wicker square. He said to Burke: "Steward, please come with me." His back, as Burke and he moved away, was a bothered ramrod.

Wharton sat down in the wicker chair with a macabre sort of pleasure. "There are," he explained, "so few novel thrills in life that even a tepidly vicarious one is acceptable." He arranged folds of his silk dressing gown carefully about pajamaed legs. He leaned backwards. He said: "If I stretch myself a bit the little square which you cut out just fits the back of the skull. Hedglin was a taller man than I am. Shall we return to our academic corpse?"

"If you like."

"Is it not true that if the man whom Miss Singlestar saw in this chair was Hedglin, and Hedglin was dead, then Hedglin or his body was concealed on the yacht when we sailed, and his murderer was temporarily interrupted by Miss Singlestar from throwing the body over the side?"

Valcour's smile continued pleasant. "Yes, Mr. Luke," he said.

"The murderer completed his mission after Miss Singlestar had left. That, too, is obvious. Mr. Valcour, who was the person who posed as Hedglin when Hedglin presumably went, and stayed, ashore?"

"Just so."

"I am being stupid. If you knew that, you would have solved the case."

"It isn't that that bothers me."

Wharton was mildly astonished. "Isn't it really?"

"I am wondering whether that person returned and is still with us."

"Who else on earth would have dumped the body?"

"If there was," Valcour said, "a body."

"If Hedglin didn't go ashore."

"If he did."

"If Miss Singlestar—"

"If she didn't." Valcour's laugh was genuine. "Our case is a squirrel cage." He added casually: "What woke you, Mr. Luke?"

Wharton didn't answer for a minute. Then he smiled broadly. "Am I Suspect Number One?"

"Heavens, no, we haven't any suspects. We haven't even a substantiated crime. Were you asleep? I'm just wondering what woke you. Some sound?"

"Sound, my dear Valcour? It must have been something cataclysmic."

"That's just what I'm getting at. The ordinary run of ship noises wouldn't have bothered you."

"It could not have been the running in the passage—"

Valcour said sharply: "What running?"

"I haven't the remotest idea. As I woke, I'd an impression that someone was running along the passage."

"Going fore or aft?"

"Not being in my usual state of mental brilliance at the moment, I couldn't say. I wake up badly. It takes a long time and leaves a bad taste in my head, rather than in my mouth. It wasn't the running that woke me. I was almost awake when I heard that. The sound that woke me came through an open porthole at the head of my bed."

"Could it, Mr. Luke, have been a splash?"

Wharton smiled thinly. "Quite easily, because it was a splash."

"Could you testify to that?"

"My dear Valcour, I could testify to anything. I haven't a single moral fiber in my entire body. It's such a nuisance. I am never quite sure when I am being wicked, and always require the reactions of an audience for a gauge."

"Your cabin is the farthest forward on the starboard side, isn't it?"

"Yes. It's the farthest from Anthony's. He would seclude me entirely if he could, and only let me out when necessary. When necessary," Wharton added, standing up and attending to the folds of his dressing gown before tightening its belt, "to him. I don't know anything about the darkest hour being just before the dawn, but I do know it's the coldest."

"Shall we locate your ports along the deck here?"

"I was about to do so from the inside and return to bed. I've a feeling I shall miss breakfast. Anthony is never quite certain whether it annoys him more to have me there or not. It's one of the minor tragedies in his life that I cannot arrange to be in two places at the same time."

"You irritate him?"

"Mentally and morally. He puts up with it because it amuses him to believe that he irritates me more so, financially."

"And does he?"

"He does. And here are my ports. If the noise that woke me was a splash, and I am increasingly certain that it was, then the body must have been put over the rail somewhere near here."

"Did you get out of bed to see what the splash was, Mr. Luke?"

"Good Lord, no."

"Why did you get out of bed?"

"My dear Valcour, have you paid any special attention to Captain Jorgensen's voice?"

"It's rather loud."

"It's very loud. It's the ideal sort of voice for getting people out of beds. I heard him talking with Anthony in the passage. The word 'hallucinations' sounded amusing. I got up and found Burke looking for corpses. He seemed increasingly upset at not finding one. He's the sort of man who likes to be obliging and get what he's sent for."

Valcour was studying the rail with a flashlight. "There are no traces here," he said.

"Of blood?"

"Of anything."

"I see that you use a magnifying lens. It's most disillusioning. I have always believed that detectives were supposed to and didn't."

Wharton started to move away, toward the door just a few feet forward which led into the saloon, and Valcour said casually: "I wonder whether you'd tell me, Mr. Luke, just why you went through Mr. Hedglin's bags."

Wharton stood quite still. "How did you know I had?"

"It was you who told me that he hadn't taken his set of razors."

Wharton's voice was slow. "You don't forget things, do you?"

"Myself, and the elephant."

"That isn't true, you know."

"I know. But it's accepted as true."

"Elephants do forget, or rather they don't remember, which isn't the same thing at all. I think that the cachet of an infallible memory is now popularly bestowed on monkeys."

Valcour said again: "Why did you go through the bags?"

"For the express purpose of reading a certain report."

"And did you?"

"It wasn't there."

"Should it have been?"

"Yes, it should have been there."

"A report on what?"

"On a person."

"Will you give me the name?"

"With pleasure. The report concerned Horatio Barlowe."

"I see."

"If you will permit me to say so, I don't believe you do. Good-night, Mr. Valcour."

"Good-night, Mr. Luke."

CHAPTER TWELVE

MOTHER AND SON

Valcour followed slowly after Wharton. He was trying to go back, mentally, to the approximate moment when Wharton had been wakened by the splash. Shortly after two. Valcour had been sitting then in his cabin at a desk by one of the two ports, and the ports had both been open. He could remember hearing no splash, no sound at all beyond faint creakings of the yacht's complaining joints and the steady press of waters.

There had been no footsteps heard along the deck which ran outside the ports. But there had been footsteps faintly audible in the passage. Running in the passage. Running aft along the passage past his door. Valcour had been curious about them and had opened the door and stared along the empty passage. He had wondered into which cabin the faint and hurrying footsteps had gone. He wondered now.

Valcour went though the empty saloon, dimly lighted by a single and ineffective lamp, and into the passage. It was empty. It was, he thought, always empty. He checked the cabin doors off as he started along it aft: Wharton Luke's on his left, Peter Moore's on his right; then his own on his left, and Horatio Barlowe's on his right—Horatio Barlowe, whose laugh was deep and soft and hearty, and whose pleasant, large face seemed singularly familiar; John Bettle's door, then, on his left, with Miss Singlestar's upon his right... John Bettle, Anthony's son, draped at the piano, hot-eyed, while Carlotta had played strange dissonances strangely... Valcour rapped lightly on John Bettle's door. There was no answer.

The next and last door on the left belonged to the large cabin used by Helen Bettle, while the next door on the right opened into Freda's room, with the last door on the right belonging to Carlotta. The door directly at the end of the passage opened into Anthony Bettle's suite.

Valcour rapped again, more sharply, on John's door. Helen Bettle's opened and John looked out. He said to Valcour: "You want me? I'm in here with Mother. Come in."

Valcour went into Helen Bettle's cabin. She was sitting dressed in a plainish wrapper in an armchair, with her hands placidly folded on her lap. They were smooth, soft, plump little hands and had no rings beyond a plain gold band. She said in her curiously tranquil voice: "John is so excited about all this, Mr. Valcour. I think it's too confusing. I am glad that Wharton is too sleepy to talk about it. I suppose Anthony is with Carlotta. Poor Miss Singlestar! She is the sort of woman who upsets so easily. Do you think she is mad?"

"She must be," John said. "Don't you think so, Mr. Valcour? Won't you sit down?"

"Thank you." Quite like his father's, John's voice was, only more eager, more excited, but equally upon the surface. John, too, Valcour thought, lived in private places, as his father lived, and he wondered whether they were the same. He sat in an armchair and said to Helen Bettle: "I don't think Miss Singlestar is mad at all. Is there any reason why we should?"

John's hair was blond, as Anthony's must have been before it turned gray, and John's features were rather an accurate replica. He said: "We don't mean mad, really. Not lunatic, you know. But seeing things?"

"The way Carlotta Balfé sees things?"

"Oh, that!"

Helen Bettle said placidly: "Anthony is so peculiar about things like that. He is so levelheaded usually. Of course, when you think of Sir Oliver Lodge and of Conan Doyle—John agrees with me rather than with Anthony, don't you, dear?"

"You bet!"

"I suppose that they really have made it important, Mr. Valcour, don't you think?"

"The psychic, Mrs. Bettle?"

"The psychic. Conan Doyle and Sir Oliver Lodge. Wharton says they've made it less tambourine. He says he wants to believe in it because he hates to think of death making him speechless. He says he'd really rather not die. Half the time I don't think he knows what he's talking about."

"You bet he does!"

"You think so, dear?"

John said abruptly: "What was it you wanted to see me about, Mr. Valcour?"

"Just a few generalities. You were asleep when all this happened?"

"Yes."

"What woke you?"

"Jorgensen's voice woke me. He was talking in the passage with Father."

"You remember hearing nothing before then?"

"No. Was there something?"

"I'm trying to check up on a splash."

Helen Bettle was almost visibly shocked. "Splash? Body?"

"Mr. Luke also heard Captain Jorgensen's voice, but he believes that some other sound woke him up before then. He thinks it was a splash."

They both said: "Oh, Wharton!" with the same odd inflection. Nothing mattered to them that Wharton said.

John went on: "The steward has told us, Mr. Valcour, that nobody's overboard and nobody's hurt." (John was, Valcour thought, so much older than his years, as an only child is so liable to be when brought up intimately with his parents, or with tutors and older people. John was nicer, Valcour decided, than his father. More likable, and more human.) "It does seem more sensible just to think that Miss Singlestar saw a man asleep in a chair."

Valcour asked him, as he had asked Anthony Bettle, "What man?"

"Why, anyone."

Helen said vaguely, gently: "John thinks it was Horatio Barlowe. He thinks you're on board, Mr. Valcour, because of Freda."

"Mother!"

She said: "You said so, dear."

"I say lots of things that don't mean anything really. Everyone says things they don't really mean, don't they, Mr. Valcour?"

"Only too frequently."

"See, Mother?"

Helen shrugged the entire business away, as she shrugged most things away which distressed her by making her think.

"Just as you say, dear. Although I don't know why you should say things you don't mean. I know I don't. It isn't as if you were interested in Freda."

"I am interested in Freda."

This jolted her. She said almost stupidly: "In Freda?"

"Yes, in Freda."

They ignored Valcour completely, absorbed in each other, in this sudden realization between them about Freda, this quickly new importance of Freda in the mutual relation of their lives.

Helen was frightened. "Are you engaged to her?"

John's voice touched the belligerent. "No, I'm not. But I want to be. I'm going to be."

The belligerence stunned her. This turning, the sudden unexpected-
ness of it. She started to cry, while her voice did not alter its placidity.
"She's a very nice girl. I don't see why you think Mr. Valcour is aboard
about her. I must talk with her. I don't know her. We don't know anything
about her. It's so difficult to associate red hair with convents."

"It's a different red. It's a very different red."

"Yes, dear. Anthony always smiles when he speaks about Horatio
Barlowe. Anthony knows something that he doesn't say. My handkerchief, dear—you'll find it on the dresser—thank you. It's always so
surprising when people want to marry." She looked suddenly very frightened indeed. "Have you said anything to your father?"

"It's hardly the right time to say things to Father."

"I should wait if I were you. This whole astonishing cruise—I wonder how it will end. Anthony's so sure about it. About its ultimate goodness. What does Freda say?"

John said with badly controlled impatience: "Say? How could she
say anything yet? She doesn't know. *I* didn't know until just now."

"Know what, dear?"

He almost shouted: "That I love her," and suddenly grew aware of
Valcour. He said: "I don't know why you were let in for this, Mr. Valcour.
We're normally quite pleasant people, and don't go in for jawing."

"Jawing? John, dear!" Helen felt better for her tranquil crying, and
wiped her eyes, which were dry.

"Well, we have been jawing. And Freda didn't go to a convent. She
went to Miss Ketcham's. That's the best girls' school in the city."

Helen brightened visibly. "I know it is, dear. Did she really? An-
nie Stewart's girl is there now. I wonder whether she and Freda know
each other. Really. Miss Ketcham's." Her pendulum swung slowly back
again. "I'm sure Mr. Valcour couldn't possibly be on board about any
girl of Miss Ketcham's."

Valcour said: "I'm not." He added pleasantly to John: "Why do you
think I should be?"

John flushed easily. His face was an angry red. "Must we go into that
again?" he said.

"But we haven't. We haven't been into it at all."

"I told you, Mr. Valcour, that I didn't mean it. That it was just something I said without meaning it. You agreed that people do."

"That is all there is about it?"

"That's all."

Helen said: "Then you don't believe Carlotta, dear?"

John said at the top of his lungs: "I don't! I never did! I don't!"

The shout set Helen's eyes swimming again. It annoyed her dreadfully when people shouted. She said: "But we *don't* know anything about her mother."

John kept right on shouting. He was bitterly excited. He said: "Who cares?"

"But John, dear, if she *was* a pickpocket."

He said: "Shut up!" He said it viciously. Bitterly. He turned to Valcour. "Don't listen to her."

Helen flinched visibly. She flinched and grew white, very bloodless. She said to John: "You're tired, darling. Go back to bed."

John's hot eyes cleared a little. He stared at his mother. He went over and kissed her. "Goodnight, Mother."

"Good-night, dear."

CHAPTER THIRTEEN

A GUN AND BOLTED DOOR

Mr. Harold Meddletree, the *Crusader*'s wireless man, adjusted the headset more comfortably upon his somewhat prominent ears. Hot and uncomfortable they got (the headphones) after wearing them for an uninterrupted stretch, and his wrist watch showed him it was half-past three. He was very much up. Nobody had asked him to stay up, but that magical (to him) rapport which had sprung into being between the yacht and New York City's police department had kept him bright-eared on the job. He was pleasantly startled from sundry reveries by a knock on the wireless-room door. He was still more pleasantly excited when it opened and Valcour came in.

"Still on the job?" Valcour said.

"I thought there might be something coming through, sir." Meddletree added happily: "From headquarters."

"That was good of you." Valcour carefully closed the door.

"Do you want a call, Mr. Valcour?"

"If you please."

"The commissioner?"

"Yes. The commissioner is an odd man. He has a passion for being got out of bed at half-past three in the morning."

Young Meddletree smiled agreeably, and started doing things with the control panel. "You'll want to phone, Mr. Valcour?"

"If it is convenient." Valcour stared around the room. There were two doors in it: the one he had just closed, which opened onto the deck, and another door in the wall that faced it. "What door is that?" he said.

"My sleeping quarters, sir."

"Have they another door opening onto the port deck?"

"Yes, sir."

"I wonder, Mr.—"

"Meddletree, Mr. Valcour."

"I wonder, Mr. Meddletree, whether it would be possible, after the connection is made, for you to leave me alone in here? I could call you when the commissioner and I were finished."

Young Meddletree looked obviously disappointed. He said: "Why, of course, sir."

"Then if you would be so kind? In our business we have to be as confidential and mysterious as possible, or the taxpayers would never believe that they were getting their money's worth. It's our only defensive armor against our general state of complete bewilderment."

Meddletree said gallantly: "Oh, I guess you don't mean that, sir."

"Then you're a very poor guesser." Valcour studied a photograph, framed, hanging on the wall beside the control panel. It was the portrait of a girl, not especially pretty, but very wholesome and very young. He liked her eyes. He said: "Your girl?"

Meddletree blushed with pleasure and pulled a wrong switch, which he promptly rectified before the man in the shore station was completely deafened into hysterics. "Yes, sir. Her name's Anna Brown. She lives in Yonkers."

"I like her eyes. There's a lot in people's eyes."

"She has got nice eyes. We hope to get hitched after this trip."

"Let me wish you happiness and luck."

"Thank you, sir… Hello? Hello?… Say, lay off, will you? I couldn't help it, could I?… Snap out of it, Sister… You're a sister… Sure, I know you got ears… Hello? Police headquarters? The yacht *Crusader* speaking… Yes, sir. Lieutenant Valcour is…"

Valcour went over to the wireless room's single port and closed it. He drew its curtains across the glass.

"All ready, Mr. Valcour."

"Thank you."

He took the receiver from young Meddletree, who at once hurried into his sleeping quarters and closed the connecting door.

"Valcour?" The commissioner's voice was sleepy.

"Sorry to get you up, Commissioner."

"Up? I wish you had. I haven't been to bed. I hope you've broken something."

"I have. Hedglin sailed. He was either dead when we sailed and his body was concealed, or else he was killed after we got under way. His body was dumped over the side at two o'clock this morning."

"Well, that's a relief." The commissioner's laugh was short and weary. "You know what I mean. Who did it?"

"God knows."

"Well, that's up to you."

"Not entirely."

"Of course not." The commissioner's yawn must have been jaw-cracking. "I'm dead for sleep, Valcour. What do you want us to do here?"

"I'd like you to get the following information at Hedglin's office, if you can."

"Long?"

"Pretty long."

"Wait until Swiggins cuts in on the other phone."

Swiggins was the commissioner's secretary.

"All right, Commissioner?"

"Yes. Swiggins is set. Go ahead."

"Hedglin is conducting some investigation for Bettle. Bettle shies at telling me what it is. Try and find out at Hedglin's office. The man who impersonated Hedglin and pulled that taxicab business took Hedglin's briefcase ashore with him. There probably was an important report or a valuable paper of some description in the briefcase. Unless Hedglin typed it himself—he uses a portable—his secretary probably knows what it is and ought to be made to talk. It's important for us to know."

"All right. Swiggins has that down."

"I'd like a man and his daughter looked up. They're both on board here. His name is Horatio Barlowe, capital b-a-r-l-o-w-e. According to Bettle, Barlowe's New York address is the Ritz Towers. He's about five feet eight inches tall, around fifty years old, weighs close on two hundred, plump, ears flat against head and smallish lobes, double chin, size sixteen collar, fullish lips, medium broad nose, eyes spaced rather close, the left eye is a shade lighter blue than the right eye, and the left lid is held a fraction closed, gray hair worn pompadour, walks with an easy balance on balls of feet and fiddles with things in his right-hand trouser pocket. O.K.?"

"Absolutely. He sounds like a highly suspicious character and will bear, as better detectives than we are are so fond of saying, watching."

"The daughter's name is Freda. She graduated recently from Miss Ketcham's. Nineteen, five foot four, one hundred and twenty pounds, copper-red hair, small well-modeled ears, sensitive mouth, largish well-spaced violet-colored eyes, no noticeable mannerisms."

"She sounds like a raving beauty."

"She is. Her mother, incidentally, may have been a pickpocket."

"That will please Miss Ketcham. The old buzzard will jump through the roof. Anything else?"

"Yes. There's another woman for investigation. She calls herself Carlotta Balfé, capital b-a-l-f-e. The e is accented acutely. For all of me it may very well be her own name. Heavens knows what nationality it's supposed to be."

"Probably Esperanto."

"She's in the twenties, five foot six, one hundred and twenty pounds, black hair, black deep-set eyes, ear lobes longish, aquiline nose, thin, perfectly carved lips. She's a determined poseur, her pet one being what ought to be known as the pretrance stage. Bettle says her city hangout is the Shelton. She's a medium."

"Is that a brilliant deduction or a fact?"

"It's her own frank confession. She says she doesn't get paid for it, so she must do it for her own amazement."

"Fat chance."

"A very fat chance. That's the list. Anything at your end, Commissioner?"

"Nothing—wait a minute."

"Yes?"

"There's a report here—here it is. A rowboat has been reported stolen from the dock alongside the yacht-club wharf at Twenty-third Street. The boat was there at six o'clock in the evening, and wasn't there at one o'clock this morning. Any hook-up?"

"Possibly. The man who impersonated Hedglin may have stolen it to get back to the yacht with before we sailed, rather than use the tender. That's a nice idea."

"It's a very nice idea. But don't they keep a man on guard by the accommodation ladder when they're in port?"

"There are several ways of getting on board besides using the accommodation ladder."

"Such as?"

"The anchor chain. It wouldn't have taken any trapeze work. Anyway, the freeboard isn't much. If the rowboat turns up I'd have it looked over."

"We will. If we find any false whiskers we'll let you know."

"By the way, Commissioner, I'd be vague about all this with the press."

"Why so?"

"Because we've only one witness who saw Hedglin on board at two o'clock, and the circumstances may have been such that her evidence may turn out to be unreliable."

"In what way?"

"The light was bad. She had just stumbled and may have been a little excited and confused. She recognized that the man in the chair was dead, which further upset her."

"Who's she and what man?"

Valcour introduced the commissioner to Miss Singlestar and gave him her version of the finding of Hedglin, as well as her story about the spot of blood on the back of the chair. He added Wharton's testimony as to having heard a splash. He touched briefly on the water spots on the rug in Hedglin's cabin, and on the fingerprintless carafe with its refilling of tap water. He spoke of the note and the fingerprintless keys of the portable typewriter.

The commissioner said: "But all this leaves us in as great a mess as ever."

"Doesn't it?"

"We had better keep right on looking for Hedglin right here in the city. On a chance."

"I would."

"Any idea what's in back of it all, Valcour?"

"None, Commissioner."

"Well, keep digging. We'll get busy at our end the first thing in the morning. In, in other words, a couple of hours from now."

"Thank you, Commissioner."

"Good-night, Valcour."

"Good-night."

Valcour replaced the receiver. He turned toward the door connecting the wireless room with the operator's quarters. It was open. Not much, but an inch or two of space showed between it and the jamb. He went to it quickly and opened it wide. Young Meddletree was flat on his face on the cabin's floor. Valcour turned him over and felt his pulse. It was beating strongly. He took a carafe and splashed water on Meddletree's face.

"What happened?" Meddletree said.

"Don't you know?"

"No."

"Have you got a gun?"

Meddletree stood up and delicately fingered a swelling lump on the back of his head. He looked less dazed. He said: "I'll admit I was listening, Mr. Valcour. I had my ear against the door. Something hit me."

Valcour said again: "Have you got a gun?"

"Why, yes."

"Then keep it with you. When you sleep, bolt both the doors."

CHAPTER FOURTEEN

TO PREVENT AND PUNISH HARM

Valcour went to the bridge, from where the *Crusader*'s searchlight no longer shafted over the waters. She had turned and was back upon her course again, heading once more for the Ragged Island of Jumentos Cays, finished with the futile search for Waverly Hedglin's body.

Gathered, leaning on the dodger, were Captain Jorgensen, First Officer Jones, and Burke. Three blacknesses against a graying east.

Valcour joined them and said to Captain Jorgensen: "Your wireless man has just been attacked. Someone struck him on the head."

They stared at Valcour, confused by their several reactions to the news. Captain Jorgensen's great bulk seemed to shrink a little, and a haggardness was faint on his face. Burke drew his breath in with a soft hiss.

Mr. Jones was the least affected of the three. He said: "It he all right now?"

"Yes, Mr. Jones. He is all right now."

Burke said: "It ain't healthy, this cruise. Take it from me, gentlemen, this cruise ain't healthy. If you want to know what I think about it, I think it's unhealthy. There's some of us in for being murdered in our beds."

Mr. Jones, who hadn't seen his bed all night, said: "Not at this rate."

"Gentlemen!" Captain Jorgensen's strong voice was uncertain. "I am a worried man, Valcour. We have searched the water and have found no body. The steward, with several men, has searched the ship and has found nothing. I was about to be serene again, when you come to me with this news. Who hit Sparks and why?"

"He doesn't know, Captain. I think it was someone who wanted to overhear my conversation with the police commissioner." Valcour explained the circumstances. He said: "Doesn't it seem the sensible thing to you for us to put back to New York and stay there until we get to the bottom of this matter and clear it up?"

"Yes, Valcour, it does. I agree that it does." Captain Jorgensen sighed prodigiously. "But can you move an unwilling stone?"

"If the leverage is strong enough."

"But is it?"

Valcour knew only too well what Captain Jorgensen meant: would a leverage of a water-spotted rug, a carafe full of tap water, a fingerprint-less typewriter keyboard, the testimony of an unstrung woman that she had seen a man sitting in a chair and thought he was dead, her own and Captain Jorgensen's testimony that a little spot that might have been blood had been seen by them on the back of the wicker chair and which was no longer there, Wharton Luke's assertion that he had been awak-ened by the sound of a splash, a wireless man who had been struck by someone on the head—would such a leverage be enough?

Valcour felt that it would be for an ordinary man. But Anthony Bettle was not an ordinary man. He was a power obsessed with a compelling mission, a mission that so very obviously fogged his perception of any-thing that did not touch upon the mission intimately. Valcour felt a ruth-lessness in Bettle, a metal tank lumbering along on expensive tractors toward some distant goal regardlessly. He said: "Couldn't you turn back on your own authority, Captain?"

"I could not, Valcour, unless the safety of the vessel were menaced and my opinion told me we should put back in order to prevent a mari-time disaster. Such a condition does not exist."

"We have passed the jurisdiction of the land?"

"Dear man, we are on the high seas."

"It is in your province, is it not, to investigate this attack upon your wireless operator?"

"It is and it will be done."

"You have the right to prevent and punish harm to everyone on board?"

"To prevent and to punish." Captain Jorgensen shrugged. "You must understand that on a yacht my hands are a little bound. On a passenger boat or a merchant vessel things would be different." He said abruptly: "Valcour, I am glad that you sailed with us. I could not understand it at first, and thought it stupid. I cannot understand anything now, but I do not think it stupid. Such businesses, such hittings, such disappearances, you know about. They are familiar to you as, to me, is the sea. We will help you while you do everything you can."

"Thank you, Captain."

Captain Jorgensen felt much better with this shifting, as it were, of the weight that had depressed so confusingly his unfamiliar shoulders. He was all set for immediate action. "What will we do now?"

"I would suggest checking up on the crew, especially in regard to this business of the wireless man. Find out as closely as you can where each man was. Did any of you notice anyone, by the way, on the port side of the boat deck within the past ten minutes?"

"No. It is too bad, we did not. We were talking here, we three. As for the helmsman it would be his business to keep his eyes on the card. In any case he could not see the deck."

"Who else have cabins on the port side besides the wireless man?"

"Mr. Jones, his cabin comes next. Mr. Jones, he has been standing here for the past quarter of an hour with me. Next to his cabin is that of the second officer's whom I do not think you have met. His name is Doorn, Walter Doorn. He is asleep. The other three doors after his are the baths, the mess, and the pantry. You will question Doorn?"

"Yes, Captain. In regard to your personnel, do you know them? Have they sailed with you before?"

"Valcour, you do not understand the business about this yacht. It is especially inserted in the Articles that there is to be no smoking aboard. It is impossible to keep a crew for more than one voyage where there is no smoking. As it is, we have to make replacements in every port we touch. It would be highly astonishing to you to know the amount of trouble such a thing as tobacco can make when you cannot have some."

"How about your officers, Captain?"

"Mr. Jones, he has been with me for two trips; the steward for six."

Burke looked smug. (He knew a good berth when he found one, and what were electric fans for anyway, if not to clear the smoke out from a cabin through an open port?) He said: "I really don't mind not smoking a bit, sir. Taking it by and large it's a nasty habit."

"Well, I do," said Jones. "I mind it. But I mind not feeding my wife more than I do not smoking a cigarette."

"You see, Valcour? It is just that way with me." Captain Jorgensen mumbled hastily: "But in my case it is not a wife. Just the same it is an obligation. As to Mr. Doorn, this is his first trip. I know nothing about him. He is a good man on his job, otherwise he does not say much and I think that he is sour. MacGregor, the chief engineer, and his assistant, Murphy, they have been with us as long as the steward. The wireless man, he is new. Mrs. Wiggins, the stewardess, she is new. I do not like that woman, Valcour, one bit. I am unhappy every time I see her. I think, when I see her face, that she has eaten some nails."

"How many men are there in the crew, Captain?"

"Four in the deck department, three in the engineer's, and three in the steward's. Ten. Ten men, two deck officers, two engineers, the steward, the stewardess, the wireless man and myself. In all, eighteen."

"That's a good-sized crew for a yacht, isn't it?"

"It is no more than enough. She is a big yacht. She is a good yacht. As a ship, I like her. She is well found." Captain Jorgensen was feeling ever so much better. His enthusiasm over the *Crusader* terminated on: "She is a good girl."

"And her name," Mr. Jones muttered, "should be Carrie."

Valcour said: "When you went aft to the wicker chair with Miss Singlestar, Captain, did you pass anyone on your way along the deck?"

"Nobody, Valcour."

"When did Carlotta Balfé join you?"

"As soon as that dear little lady had fainted."

"From which direction did Carlotta Balfé come?"

"I could not say. I am confused at faintings."

"What did she say when she joined you?"

"I do not know. I think it was something about Miss Singlestar being ill. She made some question or other about her illness. Myself, I was off immediately to attend to necessary matters here on the bridge."

"Thank you, Captain. In case I don't see you gentlemen again before morning, good-night."

They echoed his good-night, and Valcour started aft along the port deck. Chartroom. Wireless man's room. First officer's room. He stopped before the next and rapped upon the door belonging to Mr. Doorn.

CHAPTER FIFTEEN

THE DIM PASSAGE IS FOG

Thin pallid rose madder washed a graying east as Mr. Doorn opened his door. Mr. Doorn in his underwear, which also served him as pajamas, was lanky and gaunt. Very whitish, his skin was, from the bottom of a copper-circled neck down, and a hollow-cheeked face was a bronze mask on plaster. "Well?" he said.

"My name is Valcour, Mr. Doorn."

"I know it is. What do you want?"

"Some information, please."

"Well?"

"Did you hear anything or notice anyone along the deck here during the past quarter of an hour?"

"I did." Mr. Doom's voice was thick and hard, as his eyes were hard, very stonelike eyes and hard. "He barged in here as if he owned the place and said he thought it was the bathroom. The bathroom's next door."

"Who barged in, Mr. Doorn?"

"That young man they call Peter Moore."

"How long ago was that?"

"It was at three-forty. I looked at my watch. What time is it now? You can figure it out for yourself."

"That would be just about a quarter of an hour ago, Mr. Doorn. How did he strike you?"

"Unfavorably. I don't like being bothered in my sleep. I don't like people who bust in on me when I'm off duty."

"I'm sorry if I disturbed you."

"So am I. Good-night."

Mr. Doorn went whitely into his cabin's shadow and shut the door.

Peter Moore. A quarter of an hour ago. Young Meddletree had been struck about a quarter of an hour ago by someone who had entered his quarters from this deck, where Peter Moore had been. Peter was Hedglin's nephew. Presumably his heir. Nephews were famous for killing uncles when they were the heirs. They were partial to it, anyway, even when not heirs. Valcour sighed and wondered whether the sour Mr. Doom's trouble was a bad digestion or a bad conscience. They reacted about the same.

He stared at magentas in the eastern sky, flushing already the intervening sea, and breathed deeply of the clear cold morning air. Pale stars died in hazing blue above him. Where did it stand now, this strange and unusual case?

Horatio Barlowe figured in a "report" and Freda's mother may have been a pickpocket.

Young Peter had been within striking distance when a blow had been struck, and Carlotta Balfé had used her handkerchief to wipe off some blood.

Wharton Luke had almost with avidity accepted the suggestion that what had wakened him had been a splash, and the antecedents of the officers and crew were largely unknown, with Second Officer Doom having either a bad conscience or indigestion, and certainly no manners.

How prejudicial manners made one. It was unquestionably so much pleasanter to hang a boor than a gentleman. Pleasanter for the hanger.

He went down to the main deck, through the saloon, into the passage, and knocked on Peter's door. Peter said: "Come in," and Valcour opened the door and went inside. Peter, fully dressed, was slumped in an armchair. His ugliness was more pronounced by an overlayer of strain.

Valcour said pleasantly: "I wonder whether you realize, Mr. Moore, that you're in a bad way."

Peter said shortly: "I'm not up to riddles."

Valcour sat down. "This isn't a riddle. The wireless man has just been struck on the head, and the second officer has reported you as having been up there at about the time that the blow was struck."

"So the obvious conclusion is that I hit him."

"Isn't it? I don't think you did."

"Why don't you?"

"Because I don't think you killed your uncle. We run into any number of killers in our business, and I don't think you would have killed him in that way."

"In other words, I'm a perfectly good killer but that particular job didn't happen to fit my technique?"

"There's no necessity for getting sore, Mr. Moore. Everyone has it in him to be a killer. I have, we all of us have. All we need are the motive, the opportunity, and the weapon with which to commit the crime. Those three things would be a common essential for all of us, but we would differ according to our several dispositions, characters, and temperaments, in our methods of carrying the crime out. You will forgive me for taking so personal and unhappy an occurrence as your uncle's death for an example?"

Peter looked quite white. "You're satisfied that he is dead, Mr. Valcour?"

"It is unreasonable to believe anything else."

Peter still slumped bigly in the chair. "We were fond of each other, in a way," he said. "Because there was nobody else for each of us to be fond of, I suppose. Maybe it wasn't fondness so much as it was habit. We were used to each other. Either one of us would leave a gap."

"There are no other close relatives, Mr. Moore?"

"No." Peter was bitter. "There's your motive, Mr. Valcour. He was a very rich man and I'm his heir."

Valcour was puzzled about Peter. He had the feeling that what was really worrying Peter wasn't this business about Hedglin at all. It was something else. Valcour found himself thinking, for no sound reason, about Freda. He said: "There is nothing to be gained by that attitude. I honestly appreciate the shock that all this has been to you."

"All right."

"You can tell me something about your uncle's physical condition, if you will."

This interested Peter. "What's that got to do with it?" he said.

"As a rule it takes less to kill a man who is physically unwell than it does to kill a man who is fit. It takes less of a shock, or a blow, less seriously vital a wound. Was your uncle healthy? Was he well?"

"He never said. I don't think we ever talked about his health."

"How old a man was he?"

"I think around sixty."

"Do you know his physician?"

"Yes, we both have Dr. Andrew when anything's the matter."

"Has he ever spoken with you about your uncle, about his general state of health?"

"No, never."

"What are his initials and his address?"

"Dr. Andrew's?"

"Yes."

"A. W., Arthur W. Andrew. He's in the Herkimer Building on Fifth. Why?"

Valcour noted the information in a small book. "I'll call him up," he said.

"Why are you making such a point of it—or my uncle's physical condition?"

"Because in spite of one contradictory fact, I don't think your uncle's death was premeditated. The contrary fact is the question of a disguise."

"What disguise?"

"The disguise used by the man who impersonated your uncle. People don't as a rule carry gray wigs around with them, convincing wigs especially. Anyone can usually spot a wig a mile off. It takes all sorts of time and a good fistful of cash to make even a passable one. And the man who impersonated your uncle emphasized the wig. He took his hat off when he entered the tender to leave the yacht, took it off on the wharf, and left it behind him in the taxicab, and no one who saw him hatless mentioned the word 'wig.'"

"Maybe it wasn't a wig."

"Maybe it wasn't. There are four people on board, that I know of, who have gray hair: Mr. Barlowe, Mr. Bettle, Mrs. Wiggins the stewardess, and Second Officer Doorn. There may be some more scattered about among the crew. I haven't seen them. Mr. Barlowe's too fat to wear your uncle's overcoat or to impersonate him in any way convincingly, and I can't picture the stewardess chinning herself up onto the deck from a rowboat or climbing up the anchor chain." Valcour added pleasantly: "All of which leaves us with the palpable fact that Mr. Bettle and Second Officer Doorn have gray hair, and we can't electrocute them for that. It also leaves us with the irritating possibility that it may actually *have* been your uncle who went ashore, and that the man whom Miss Singlestar found in the chair may have been disguised to resemble your uncle, and not have been dead at all. And God knows why."

"You said that my uncle was dead, Mr. Valcour."

"Don't think me frivolous, Mr. Moore. I'm not. I am convinced of your uncle's regrettable death. I am simply placing my views before you because you, more than anyone else, have the right to be interested in the solution of his murder." He added casually: "What brought you upon the boat deck about half an hour ago?"

"When I hit the wireless man?"

Valcour smiled back at Peter. "When you didn't hit the wireless man."

Peter said: "You can see the stars better up there."

"How long were you up there?"

"I don't know. It seemed quite a while."

"When you mistook the pleasant Mr. Doom's room for the bathroom, you were on the port side of the deck. The wireless man's door is the second one forward from Doom's. Was anyone near it? Did you see anyone at all?"

"No. No one at all."

Valcour said quietly: "Then when was it that you did see somebody, Mr. Moore?"

Peter stared at the ports, at their clear pale amber light. A sailor passed in front of them along the deck. Peter thought: *They'll be swabbing down the decks soon. The night's finished*. He said: "You misunderstood me. I said no one at all."

Valcour stood up. "Just as you wish, Mr. Moore. Good-night."

Peter looked at him oddly, intently. His lips were white. "Good-night, Mir. Valcour."

Valcour went out into the passage. It was stuffy and close in the passage, and a single overhead lamp lit it obscurely. All sounds of the ship were magnified in it, then muffled into intimacy—pulse, drive, rise, fall—pulse, drive, rise, fall—monotonous, purposeful coordination of machinery and man and sea…

He went into his cabin but did not close the door. Another one had opened, the one coming from the saloon, and Valcour saw Anthony Bettle and Carlotta coming along the passage. Washed out, weary-looking, they were. Two gentle wraiths. Carlotta's eyes were burned-out pits above a faded make-up, while Bettle's face was a cratered, grayish moon. She was leaning heavily on his arm, listless, the way dead leaves are on some slow and thoughtful river. Bettle was staring ahead along the passage, beyond its ending, straight through its ending out to some private horizon that must, from his expression, have been rimmed with dread. They went past Valcour, standing in his doorway. They went on down to Carlotta's cabin, and she went inside. They did not say good-night.

Valcour walked down toward Bettle, and Bettle stared at him blankly, as at someone entirely unfamiliar to him.

"Would it bother you very much to see me for a minute or two, Mr. Bettle?"

Bettle turned to the door of his suite and fumbled with its knob. He said: "Not now. Nothing now."

"I think it advisable."

"Advisable? Oh, yes, it's you, Mr. Valcour." Bettle took a grip on himself. Something of his dominance returned, and his voice grew clearer, more loud. "You are worried about that puzzling business of Waverly Hedglin. It is quite all right. Maybelle is going to tell Carlotta all about it. We aren't to worry."

"'Maybelle'?"

"Maybelle is Carlotta's control."

"I see." Valcour stepped quickly forward and placed a supporting hand on Bettle's arm.

"These affairs, Mr. Valcour, are quite a strain. They are naturally a dreadful strain on Carlotta. I am deeply shocked. I am shocked beyond all measure."

Valcour kept his voice suggestively low.

"Because of some information concerning Mr. Hedglin?"

"It isn't that. It is something more pressing than that. It is urgent. Imminent."

"Perhaps if you were to tell me about it?" He looked sharply into Bettle's tired eyes. They were indicative, and hinted things.

"You must say nothing about this to anyone, Mr. Valcour. As in all psychic matters, there is an element of possible error, an unclearness in the interpretation. Carlotta has been wrong before."

"She has received some message, some warning?"

"If you are not in sympathy it will be difficult for you to understand this, but I should like you to know. We may wish to call upon your help."

"There are so many unexplained things in life that it would be stupid to keep a closed mind about anything."

"Quite right. That is entirely right." Bettle sighed heavily and fumbled again with the knob. "Good-night, Mr. Valcour."

"You haven't told me yet, Mr. Bettle."

Bettle's voice was haggard, sifting thinly as weak fog through the dim-lit passage. "Maybelle said, Mr. Valcour, that at a quarter after some unspecified hour of to-morrow night Carlotta is going to be dead."

PART THREE

CHAPTER SIXTEEN

HOT SUN BRINGS NO LIGHT

Porpoises looped slickly at the bows, looping, looping, strange projectiles hurtling, all with incredible swiftness and grace, an amusing circus with the Gulf Stream for their rings. But Valcour was not amused. Sunlight sank richly with its glow and heat, jading blue water and adding soft glitter to creaming crests, but he saw no beauty in it and felt no warmth.

He thought: *Just as love makes you blind so does wealth, and of the two blindnesses wealth is the worse because of the incalculable harm it is able to do to people other than yourself.* Bettle was wealth. And Bettle was stone blind.

Valcour thought of Helen Bettle, Anthony's wife. Her dossier was familiar to him: the daughter of a spendthrift family that had been socially prominent in New York during the 'nineties, who had saved her father from an ugly financial scandal by marrying Bettle.

That, Valcour thought, had not been as tough as it might seem to be on Bettle. He had accepted the marriage with his eyes open. Helen was a good woman, she had made Bettle a good wife, she had borne him a son, and she had given him a sufficiently satisfactory standing among people whom he had wanted to know, in payment for his money. It was the old, the threadbare tale that has been time and again retold. But it had harmed Helen by turning her nature from its normal course. She should be, Valcour thought, a pleasant, jolly, somewhat stout, middle-aged woman and not the inert and tired lump of flaccidity that she was.

It had harmed the son (this wealth) and had negatived him into a weak replica of the strong original. Certainly it had chained Wharton Luke, completely sapping from him whatever of purpose for initiative living there may ever have been in him.

Barlowe, Freda, Peter, Carlotta, all of them were there because Bettle was wealth, and not because of any liking for the man. The very yacht's officers and men were not only expected to do their several duties efficiently, but their personal habits were stringently imposed upon as well. And very great wealth, such as Bettle's, gave scope to madness if, Valcour thought, you could term fanatic fervor madness. For there was decided fanaticism in the manner with which Anthony Bettle was pursuing whatever special and secret project that was hurrying him toward the Ragged Island of Jumentos Cays.

Bettle's dabbling with the psychic was not unusual. Many men of wealth and of keen mental ability did that. But Bettle's complete disinterestedness in anything that did not touch upon his project was unusual. His disinterestedness, for example, in the fate of Hedglin. Nothing bothered Bettle unless it caused a dropping of the revolutions that were propelling him toward his destination of the Ragged Island of Jumentos Cays. Valcour stopped looking at porpoises. He looked at his watch. It was ten o'clock. He started aft. He wanted to see Bettle.

He found Bettle in the living room of his suite. Bettle was a force again, pinkly shaved, very spruce, and his manner once more radiated strength and exactness of purpose. He said briskly to Valcour: "Good-morning, Mr. Valcour. I am glad you came in. I wanted to talk to you about last night. You are interested in psychology? Of course. Men who rise to your position in your profession are interested in it of necessity. You appreciate the overemphasis which night places on all emotions."

"Because the eye is less distracted with outward and physical things. Introspection almost becomes a necessity."

"Exactly. Do sit down. And if we permit ourselves to give sway to those emotions the effect of them is all the more emphatic. A refreshing sleep and subsequent daylight dilute their strength most noticeably. I want you to forget our little talk in the passage."

"You are not so much impressed with it as you were then?"

The subject had pointedly grown distasteful to Bettle. He said: "As I explained to you, Mr. Valcour, Carlotta is not infallible. Every person makes mistakes in his own profession. It is stupid to expect perfection."

Valcour was deliberately blunt: "Then you are satisfied that there is nothing in Miss Balfé's belief that she is going to die to-night?"

"Quite satisfied. The idea is absurd." (Valcour had the feeling that anything which interfered with Bettle's plans would seem absurd to Bettle. Carlotta's death would interfere, in the sense that Bettle so obviously used her as a satisfactory and occult yes-man. Therefore Carlotta was not to be dead.) Bettle went on: "Why should she die? Carlotta is a young and healthy woman."

"Mr. Hedglin was not old and was, so far as I have been able to find out, a perfectly healthy man."

"There is no connecting link."

"Forgive me for staying on the subject, Mr. Bettle, but isn't there? I understood from what you said last night that while Miss Balfé was in rapport with her control the question of Mr. Hedglin's disappearance was touched on. Was there anything definite said?"

"Nothing, Mr. Valcour. Nothing at all. We were advised not to worry and that everything would be explained to us later."

"But isn't that contradictory?"

"I fail to see why."

Valcour said patiently: "If her control told Miss Balfé that she was going to die to-night, how would it then be possible for the control later to explain to Miss Balfé about Mr. Hedglin's disappearance? Miss Balfé would be dead."

Bettle remained hardily stubborn about Carlotta's possible deadness. He said: "Let me make myself very plain, very explicit. Carlotta's control does not come right out and say: *In two hours from now you will receive a letter.* She does not say things clearly in ABC language like that. Her statements are obscure, as were those of the Delphic and other oracles. They require interpretation, and more often than not they are subject to a double interpretation that might seem upon its surface to be contradictory. In regard to Carlotta's death I am satisfied that the wrong interpretation was applied." Bettle's manner said: *So let us have no more stupidness about Carlotta's death.*

"How does Miss Balfé feel about it?"

"I haven't seen Carlotta. She is not up yet. There is naturally a reaction of exhaustion after such a protracted séance as we held last night. But I feel sure she will agree with me. She has generally conceded that I have been right, in any argument that has risen between us, and events have subsequently proven it in most cases. So I repeat my request, Mr. Valcour, that you will forget our little talk in the passage."

"Certainly, Mr. Bettle."

"Thank you."

Bettle's bow implied: *Then that is all. If you will be so good as to leave me, I will busy myself with my own devices.*

Valcour did not move from his chair. "There is one point in this case," he said, "that touches you directly. I am again referring to Mr. Hedglin's disappearance."

Bettle was interested. "Yes?"

"Mr. Hedglin, or else the man who impersonated him, took a briefcase ashore. That briefcase is gone."

"Well?"

"I understand from statements made by Mr. Hedglin to his nephew that the briefcase contained dynamite, some information or report that touched upon an investigation which Mr. Hedglin was making for you. Mr. Hedglin made an odd remark which his nephew remembered. He said that most illusions were nothing more than delusions. He said that you were going to be deeply upset."

Bettle relaxed. He said again, indifferently: "Well?"

"The fact doesn't trouble you?"

"What fact, Mr. Valcour?"

"Your ignorance as to the nature of the report's contents."

Bettle stood up. "I am not ignorant of its contents. I think I know exactly what information the report contained." His smile was very smug. "I am not a man, Mr. Valcour, who places all of his eggs in one basket."

Valcour stood up, too. "Have you an authentic sample of Mr. Hedglin's signature?" he said.

This was confusing. "Yes. Why?"

"I want to compare it with the signature on the note that Mr. Hedglin left for you."

Bettle walked impatiently to a desk and took some letters from a drawer. "Here's one," he said. "Here's another."

Valcour went with the letters to strong sunlight streaming through a port. He took Hedglin's note from his pocket and with the magnifying lens compared the signatures. "In my opinion the signature on this note is a forgery," he said.

"You are an expert on calligraphy, Mr. Valcour?"

"No."

"Then you will yourself admit that your opinion is open to doubt. I am not being intentionally rude. I just wish to balance the other end of the scale. Your profession naturally leads you toward taking the—well, shall we say the darker view of things?"

Like a fissureless wall, Bettle was, confident in its highness, its smooth impregnability, and Valcour was willing to concede the futility of butting his head up against it. Many people were like that, like Bettle. The whole state of Missouri was reputed to be. Show Bettle a wounded or an injured body and he would accept it as a fact that murder or suicide had been done. Show him a sheet of flame and he'd accept it as danger and would turn back. But conjectural deductions were useless as a means of convincing him, unless he could employ their implications to further his own private ends.

Valcour returned Hedglin's letters. He put the questioned note back in his pocket. He said: "I shan't disturb you again unless some news comes to me from the commissioner that requires your attention."

"You mustn't think me unsocial, Mr. Valcour." Bettle, having made his point, was quite willing to be pleasant. "My mind is filled with important details. I frequently must concentrate for long periods of time." *And this*, his bow hinted, *is such a time*. He was staring absently at a combination ship's clock-and-barometer set on his desk. He said sharply: "That's bad."

"What is bad, Mr. Bettle?"

"The glass is falling. We'll be in for a slant of bad weather." Bettle was suddenly savage. "It is delays of that nature, delays over which I have no control, which are so infuriating. The others…"

"Yes?"

Like a cold cutting wind, Bettle's voice was. "I am thoroughly capable of controlling any form of human delay, Mr. Valcour."

The passage door opened violently and Carlotta was in the room with them, saying harshly to Bettle: "We must talk, we must discuss this thing at once."

"Mr. Valcour is just going, Carlotta."

Valcour went out by the open passage door. He closed it. His eyes were filled with Carlotta, with her blazing dejection. Through the panels, he heard Bettle's lowering voice say: "There'll be no more of this. I warn you, Carlotta, there's a limit to…"

Wood dulled the rest.

CHAPTER SEVENTEEN

MRS. WIGGINS HAD A BATH

Captain Jorgensen was also uneasy about the weather. "I have a feeling," he said as Valcour joined him on the bridge, "that some real hard weather will shortly commence."

Valcour stared at a cloudless sky, felt the heat of a burning sun. He said: "All of which goes to prove how little I know about the sea. To-day looks to me like a good one for anybody's picnic."

"There is too much humidity. I am not satisfied with the glass. We are approaching a bad storm area at a bad season of the year."

"It would take a pretty severe storm to bother a yacht of this size, wouldn't it?"

"My worry is not of her. With sufficient warning ahead of time I would not worry too much about her even in a hurricane. It is the conditions on board that would be unpleasant." He sighed gustily. "But all that lies in the laps of the gods. They are very full places, Valcour—the laps of the gods. I hope that I am wrong and that the indications will clear. I should not like my mind annoyed by weather when it has all this other stuff upon it. We have made a check-up of the crew and everyone was where he should be, or else with somebody else, when Sparks was struck last night." Captain Jorgensen added with heavy impartiality: "We must except the chief engineer, Mr. MacGregor, and Mr. Doom. They were both in their cabins. MacGregor says he slept, and Mr. Doom tells me that he would have slept if he had been let."

Valcour said reflectively: "Bettle—Luke—Barlowe—Peter—John? Mrs. Bettle—Carlotta Balfé—Freda Barlowe—Miss Singlestar? Take your choice. If we eliminate the ship's complement they're the only ones left. Unless you wish to believe that I struck the wireless man myself?"

"My dear Valcour!" Captain Jorgensen was explosive. "And surely you do not include the ladies?" The ladies, taken as a sex collectively, were automatically ruled out by Captain Jorgensen when it came to any situation not connected either with loveliness or pleasure. He did admit that they had their little flare-ups and occasional temperamental spats, but when it came to one of them socking his wireless operator on the head…

"I could tell you of one woman, Captain, whom you would call the most charming and dearest little old lady in the world. Apart from her unpleasant habit of throwing vitriol in pretty girls' faces, she was."

"Really, Valcour, you shock me. It is hard to believe that such things are so." Captain Jorgensen was seriously upset. "You do not think for one moment that that dear little Miss Singlestar—"

"Heavens, no. Not for a minute. I'm just pointing out that you can't go by sex, or age, or faces. It's the inner works that make the criminal, not the surface."

"Tell me, which one do you pick out?"

"Nobody yet. How can we? What do we know?"

"Yes, Valcour. What is it we know?"

"Very little. Around the time that Mr. Meddletree was struck, I understand that Mr. Bettle and Carlotta Balfé were closeted in the small library which is just forward of the saloon on the port side. We know that Mr. Doorn had his cabin door opened by Peter Moore. Moore claims he saw nobody on the boat deck while he was up there. I don't quite believe him. I found John Bettle and his mother in her cabin. I don't know anything about Mr. Barlowe, Mr. Luke, Freda Barlowe, or Miss Singlestar. There you are."

"But that is no place."

"No place. Captain, who checked up on the stewardess?"

"I did." Captain Jorgensen flushed uncomfortably. It was straining quite a point for him to include Mrs. Wiggins among "the ladies."

"She told me, Valcour, that she was taking a bath. She was quite nasty and bitter about it. She had a bath towel wrapped around her head, and from what I could see of her hair it was wet. Frightful. She looked frightful."

"Did she say anything about Miss Singlestar? About how long she stayed in the cabin with her, or anything?"

"I asked her that. She said that she did not stay with that dear little lady at all after she had left her at her cabin. The red-headed Miss Barlowe said that she would herself see to Miss Singlestar. There is a connecting door between their two cabins."

"So Mrs. Wiggins left Miss Singlestar right away."

"Valcour, to get her to admit anything, even the simplest thing, was like pulling nails. You would think from her manner toward me that I was using three degrees."

"If she left Miss Singlestar at once that would be shortly after two o'clock, and you couldn't have questioned her until almost a quarter to four. Her hair wouldn't stay wet for an hour and a half. She must just shortly have finished her bath when you went to her. I wonder what she was doing up to then."

From the little twistings of his face, Captain Jorgensen was thinking almost visibly. He was trying to fit Mrs. Wiggins (who still clung among "the ladies") into the possible role of a wireless-man-slugger. "She is a good strong woman," he said. "I have seen her lift a hamperful of clothes that would be a good hoist for a man." He added impulsively and with an agreeable anticipation: "Shall we clap her in irons?"

Valcour smiled. "We've only the bath against her."

"I tell you I have feelings about her. But we shall wait."

"I'm afraid we'll have to. If you will excuse me, Captain, I think I'll get in touch with the commissioner. Possibly he has turned something up at his end."

Valcour left Captain Jorgensen, who was happily revolving in his mind's eye a pleasing portrait of a manacled Mrs. Wiggins, and started aft for the wireless shack. He came upon the first officer lounging in the chartroom doorway. Mr. Jones looked gloomy. Valcour said: "Good-morning. There's something I've been wanting to ask you ever since we sailed."

Mr. Jones moved an easy step or two and shifted his gloomy lounging to the starboard rail. "It's after breakfast that I mind it most," he said.

Valcour smiled sympathetically. "Not smoking?"

"Not smoking." Mr. Jones added earnestly: "It gets on your nerves. I've known crews to go all to hell when their tobacco ran out. What do you want to ask me, Mr. Valcour?"

"I wish you would tell me, Mr. Jones, why it was that just as we were sailing you said to me: 'I'm glad you're coming,' and 'I hope you brought your gun.'"

CHAPTER EIGHTEEN

BARLOWE OWNS A PAST

Mr. Jones stared over a shoulder to assure himself that they were alone. "I've heard things, Mr. Valcour," he said. "There was a little talk in shipping circles about this cruise." He added casually: "Things leak."

"What was it you heard?"

Mr. Jones selected one of the passing waves and spat at it significantly. "You may not have noticed it, but there's a fair-sized hold just abaft the chain locker. Well, you don't find holds of that size in a private yacht as a general thing, or the type derricks that are on the forward deck, or the winches. Such fittings are for cargo."

Valcour said carefully: "There is a cargo?"

"The hold's supposed to be for planes and automobiles. Mr. Bettle, when he goes places, takes his private planes and his private automobiles. Two planes and four automobiles. It's a miracle that he knows how to walk."

"Well, doesn't that explain the hold?"

"Oh, sure." The ship's bell struck six times. "There goes eleven." Mr. Jones added, as he started to drift forward toward the bridge: "That hold isn't full of planes and automobiles this time, Mr. Valcour. It's full of copper stills."

Valcour stayed leaning against the rail and stared after the ambling Mr. Jones. Copper stills. It didn't fit. Anthony Bettle had impressed him as being a genuinely sincere man, sincere both in his principles and in his beliefs. And Bettle was strongly opposed both to tobacco and liquor. Why copper stills? Did Bettle, Valcour wondered absently, know that the cargo in the hold was copper stills? For the matter of that, did Mr. Jones know? Seamen were the worst sort of gossips. A hair was enough for them to construct a mattress with. In this instance, perhaps, a gleam of copper.

But any cargo if it were heavy and bulky enough would be unusual, unless Bettle were planning to build, to establish a little pied-a-terre on the Ragged Island of Jumentos Cays. But Bettle did not appeal to Valcour as the type of man who would run around and establish pied-a-terres on obscure and romantic islands.

Planes? A base for planes? Why?

He did wish that Bettle would loosen up and tell him what this tiresomely mysterious project was. Perhaps the commissioner had been able to get some line on it at Hedglin's office.

Hedglin...

What a baffling mess the whole Hedglin business was! Only two things were positive about it:

Hedglin was missing, and Miss Singlestar had seen a man who might have been Hedglin sitting in a chair.

And Carlotta's control had told her that at a quarter after some unspecified hour to-night Carlotta was going to be dead.

That was the most puzzling point to Valcour of all; not the statement in itself, but that Carlotta's own lips should have been the ones to make it. He wondered what her game was. It seemed absurd to think that she had really received a message, absurd to take the control Maybelle seriously, so unfortunately much of that sort of thing was purposefully faked. There were, of course, rare people who were genuinely psychic, and for whose astonishingly accurate probings into the future there had never been any adequately practical explanation. He looked at his watch. It was a quarter after eleven. He walked to the wireless-room door, opened it, and went inside.

The lump on young Meddletree's head was visibly apparent. Mr. Meddletree hadn't slept very well because of it, and his nerves were considerably upset. He had also considered it wise to sleep with the ports closed, in view of Valcour's warning about carrying a gun and bolting his doors. This had heightened his sleeplessness by making the air in the cabin close and stuffy. His views on life were circling the bilious.

"Good-morning," Valcour said. He stared at the lump. "You did get a nasty crack, didn't you?"

"I'll say I did." Meddletree's thin lips tightened. "When I catch the guy who gave it to me I'm going to sock him one on the pan even if it's old Bettle himself."

"You've been stewing about it."

"Who wouldn't? I've been stewing about it all night."

"Remember anything?"

"I've been trying to and can't. But there's one funny thing."

"What's that?"

"The deck door to my cabin's got a noisy hinge."

"Then you remember hearing it open?"

"That's just it. I would have, but I don't."

Valcour thought of this for a minute. He said: "I see."

"You want the commissioner, Mr. Valcour?"

"Please."

Meddletree fiddled with switches. "You want me to duck out again when I get him?"

"It does seem an imposition, but if you don't mind?"

"I don't mind. And you can believe me that this time I'll keep my eyes open." Meddletree busied himself with getting the connection.

Valcour said: "Tell me, you came back in here last night and turned off the set?"

"Sure."

"When?"

"Right after you'd left. The chief engineer would have raised hell with me if I hadn't. He thinks he owns all the juice on this ship. And for all of me, he can. Of all the lousy tubs—Hello? Hello? Police headquarters? Yacht *Crusader* speaking..." He turned again to Valcour. "It'll be through now in a minute."

Valcour indicated an ornamental ashtray on the desk. "Why do you keep that there?" he said. "Isn't it unnecessarily tantalizing, or don't you smoke?"

"Sure I smoke. It drives me almost crazy right after breakfast, not to be able to. That tray is a present from the girl. She got it at Atlantic City when she was down there on an excursion this summer with her aunt. Pretty, isn't it? Her aunt runs a boarding house up on West a Hundred-and-ninety—Hello? Just a minute, please, Commissioner. O.K., Mr. Valcour."

Meddletree handed over the receiver and left the wireless room. Valcour stood so that he could watch both of its doors. "Commissioner?" he said. "Yes, Valcour. Good-morning."

"Good-morning. Any news?"

"Some just came through. I was about to call you."

"Good!"

"It's about Barlowe."

"Find him in the files?"

"There was a circular about him in the files."

"I was sure that his face was familiar."

"The real report about him, though, comes from Hedglin's office. Hedglin was looking him up for Bettle. Sounds pretty good, doesn't it? I can almost hear the clink of handcuffs."

"They don't clink, and it sounds almost too good. I still can't picture Barlowe in Hedglin's overcoat."

"Then don't try." The commissioner was feeling pleasantly exuberant, as he always did when a possible solution for an important case was in view. "Picture a henchman."

"What's Barlowe's racket?"

"Swindles."

"Any record of violence?"

"No. I wish there had been. I know the two don't go together as a rule. We can consider Barlowe the exception."

"I don't think we can. I don't think he'd hurt a fly, physically, no matter how many mites he'd squeeze out of widows."

"They weren't mites. He never dealt in less than five figures."

"Any convictions?"

"None. But there were three hung juries. He's a smart man."

"He's got a nice daughter."

"He must have, or Miss Ketcham never would have admitted her. Her record, incidentally, is as clear as a bell. We stepped pretty delicately while making inquiries at the school. When this breaks, the Ketcham's going to have a fit."

"Anything about the allegedly pocket-picking mother?"

"Can't turn up a thing, but we're still on it."

"What are the details about Barlowe?"

"Nineteen hundred and nineteen is the first, the Half-Penny Gold Mines in Arizona. The clean-up was approximated at fifty-seven thousand. Nineteen twenty-six, the Done-Well oil wells in Texas, clean-up placed at ninety thousand. Nineteen twenty-eight, back to the nuggets with the Placer mine in Saskatchewan, clean-up unknown but considered the biggest yet. The man's a mint."

"What names did he use?"

"He stuck to one. It's a peach: George Sincere. He operated entirely in the West and there never was any hook-up with his daughter or his home life in the East. All we have of him here in the files is his mug on a Wanted circular from California, issued back in nineteen twenty. What's wrong with the picture? He's after Bettle for something—probably intends making it the final haul—when along comes Hedglin, who has investigated him, rooted out his past, and is about to disclose the horrid facts to Bettle. The answer is: Barlowe blots out Hedglin."

"What good would it do him? He's smart enough to feel pretty sure there would be duplicates of Hedglin's report on him in Hedglin's office."

"My dear Valcour, you think of the most annoying things. Why not look upon life simply?"

"Because it isn't simple. No, Commissioner, I don't think Barlowe would kill Hedglin to suppress that report simply because it might interfere with his plans concerning Bettle." Valcour added slowly: "But I do think it conceivable that he'd kill Hedglin to suppress that report for the sake of his daughter—if—" (he was feeling his way among these strange conjectures uncertainly) "—if he thought there was a possibility of marriage between his daughter and Bettle's son. I know that Bettle's son is in love with her. He said so. He has said that he wants to marry her—and if that marriage could be arranged for before the duplicates came to light—That's a little far-fetched, isn't it?"

"It's plausible, Valcour. You can judge best, of course. You're on the spot and can size them up."

"And there isn't a shred of proof that Barlowe did kill Hedglin. So far as that goes, Commissioner, there isn't even any proof that Hedglin is dead."

"I know it." The commissioner was unhappily irritable. "It's a damn nuisance not having a corpse."

"Possibly Maybelle will arrange one for you to-night."

"Maybelle? And who, pray, is Maybelle or what?"

"She's a control. She's Carlotta Balfé's control. She sent Carlotta a message that at a quarter after some unspecified hour to-night Carlotta is going to be dead." Valcour went on to explain in detail about the séance last night. He touched on Bettle's reactions to it in the passage, and his later ones of the morning. "Were you able to turn up anything, Commissioner, as to Bettle's purpose in making this cruise? What his 'project' was?"

"No. There was a blank on that at Hedglin's office. We could get nothing out of them but that report about Barlowe."

"What was it, do you think, that they were holding back?"

"You feel there was something?"

"I think there must have been something."

"Sam felt that way, too. Sam covered their end. He said that Hedglin's secretary struck him as though she were holding something back. He says she's a polite, middle-aged, stubborn, chromium-plated safe. I'll get him to work on her again if you say so. He'll open her if anybody can. You think it very important?"

Valcour said: "I think it is the real reason why the briefcase was stolen. And I think it is the answer to why Hedglin was killed."

CHAPTER NINETEEN

A BOMB BURSTS MILDLY

The commissioner was impressed. He said: "Then you discount pretty heavily, Valcour, the information about Barlowe?"

"Not essentially, Commissioner, but I do feel certain that there is something else. Something we haven't been able to place a finger on as yet at all. As you may have noted, it's an odd case."

"Odd? It's as bad as a charity tableau." The commissioner sighed audibly. "Barlowe would make it so simple."

"I cannot give up the conviction that Hedglin was impersonated. It's the only rational thing to believe. And with Barlowe's figure he never could have done it. I'm not inclined toward there having been any accessories either before or after the crime. I think it's a one-man job. I also can't give up the conviction that the crime was unpremeditated, and yet, unless Bettle or Doorn or Mrs. Wiggins did it, how did the impersonator pull out of his sleeve a perfectly convincing crop of gray hair?"

"Who's Doorn? Who's Mrs. Wiggins? What about gray hair?"

Valcour explained. Then he said: "Did you line up anything on Carlotta Balfé?"

"Nothing beyond the fact that she lives circumspectly—aren't you fond of the word 'circumspectly'? I am. I've often wondered just what it means. At any rate, she lives at the Shelton and receives quite prominent people in her apartment. The management seemed surprised and a little upset at the idea that she dabbled in spiritualism. I imagine it's a little too Coney Island. She'll probably find out when she gets back that she's moved. How does she strike you?"

"She struck me this morning, Commissioner, as being a rather startled and a very worried woman."

"You're not putting any stock in this dead-on-the-quarter-hour business, are you?"

Valcour's laugh was apologetic. "I prefer to answer that question to-morrow," he said.

"Nonsense!"

"Remember the Osterholt case?"

"But in that instance the message was faked."

"Well, there's no reason why Maybelle's shouldn't have been. I haven't examined the scene of last night's séance. It took place in a small library just forward of the saloon."

"But doesn't Maybelle do all her talking via Carlotta herself?"

"There's this point to consider, Commissioner. You've run into as many mediums as I have. Personally I feel that after they've been in the game for a while, no matter how much charlatanism they use in it, there isn't one of them who doesn't get bitten."

"Bitten?"

"Yes. With doubt. With doubt as to whether there might not be something genuine in it after all. If anyone dramatizes himself for a long enough time in any role he can't help but subconsciously to live that role a little, to feel moments when he almost believes that the role is reality."

"Possibly true, Valcour, and I don't know how much money this talk is costing Bettle per minute. But what of it? Suppose Balfé is bitten?"

"It's the only explanation for her having made what would otherwise be an absurd statement. She doesn't impress me as being on the verge of committing suicide. On the contrary, up to this morning she seemed like any cat on the point of swallowing any canary."

"You seriously feel that the message may have come from her spontaneously? I refuse to say occultly."

"Either that, or else that the message may have been sent by someone else's voice after she and Bettle had worked themselves into a highly emotional state."

"And now that we're both crazy, just what do you mean by that?"

"I mean that a third person may have been concealed in the library during the séance and may have imitated Maybelle's voice and chimed in at the proper moment. Or it could have been done through a port or the door."

"But why?"

"Is it any more absurd than the supposedly established facts that Hedglin went ashore, jumped hatless and coatless out of a taxicab, was seen dead here in a chair, and eventually dissolved into what might have been a drop of blood?"

"I believe from the expression on my stenographer's face that he is convinced I've gone mad. Good-bye, Valcour. I can't stand any more just now."

"Good-bye, Commissioner. You'll put Sam right on Hedglin's secretary, won't you?"

"I will. She'll probably take off her spectacles and say: "*I'm* Waverly Hedglin, and what are you going to do about it?' Good-bye—good-bye—"

"Good-bye."

Valcour hung up. He stared sharply at the deck door. He went to it and opened it. "Good-morning, Mr. Barlowe," he said.

Barlowe's laugh was deep and slow and hearty. "You startled me, Mr. Valcour. I was about to come in."

"By all means do. I'll just let the operator know that I've finished my connection."

"Been in touch with the commissioner?"

"Yes." Valcour went to the connecting door and rapped on it. "All finished, Mr. Meddletree," he said.

Young Meddletree came out, stared for an instant at Barlowe, nodded to him, and then went over to the panel and opened switches.

"It is a fascinating, extraordinary, perfectly magical thing—wireless telephony. Don't you think so, Mr. Valcour?" Barlowe beamed largely, warmly about the room. "Black art. Not so many centuries ago its inventors would have been boiled in oil." Barlowe's beam concentrated on Mr. Meddletree. "Also its operators, young man."

Meddletree was in no good mood for airy badinage. He said: "Do you want to send a message, sir?"

"Some time. Not immediately. Whenever you are not busy."

"I'm not busy now."

"Then I will return here shortly. Just at present I am hoping that Mr. Valcour will join me for a little stroll on deck."

"Very glad to, Mr. Barlowe."

They went outside and walked aft along the deck.

"My life is a race, Mr. Valcour, between mild exercise and obesity. How perfect the air is! I understand we're already in the Gulf Stream. I've often thought it a pity that its warmth could not be commercialized." His laugh was there again. "Though it's stupid to say that—when I think of hotel bills at Bermuda or the West Indies. So you were talking with the commissioner? Is there any late news about poor Hedglin, or aren't you inclined to broadcast?"

"I wish that there were some to broadcast, Mr. Barlowe. Things are tantalizingly blank. I wonder whether you could help me."

"I shall be delighted to if I can. In what respect?"

"About last night."

"All of last night?"

"Chiefly around two o'clock. But all of it, really."

"Now let me see. Two o'clock. It's so difficult to associate a two-o'clock with any background other than a night club. I seriously believe, Mr. Valcour, that I was in bed."

Valcour smiled back agreeably. "Asleep?"

"Perhaps. The last time I noticed my watch it was half after one. I read for a little while after then."

"Notice any noises?"

"Dozens. I don't think there is anything on earth so persistently noisy as a ship in the nighttime when it's at sea. But you naturally mean anything peculiar. I don't think I did."

"When the stewardess took Miss Singlestar back to her cabin didn't it waken you? Her cabin is right next to yours, isn't it?"

"Yes, and young Moore is on the other side. No, Mr. Valcour, it didn't waken me. Nothing that I have ever known of has ever wakened me. I'm almost the perfect sleeper."

"What time did you come on board, Mr. Barlowe?"

"Early. In fact immediately after dinner, and even the dinner was early. I got here around eight."

"Your daughter came with you?"

"No. Freda followed with Miss Singlestar. I don't believe they got here until ten or ten-thirty." Barlowe added casually: "I had to come on board early in case Bettle wanted to talk anything over."

"Did he?"

"He didn't." Barlowe stopped by the starboard rail and stared speculatively across blue waters. He spoke carefully, exactly. He said: "I wanted to find out, before my daughter came on board, whether he had made a last-minute change of mind."

"About what, Mr. Barlowe?"

"About me. About still keeping me on in my job, in view of his knowledge that I am George Sincere."

CHAPTER TWENTY

RED HAIR IN SUN

Bright hot, the sun was, blazing from blue sky on bluer water, baking the deck, making lifeboats painfully white, and Freda was mounting the starboard ladder from the main deck and coming toward them with her copper-flashing hair through the whiteness and the heat.

Barlowe looked miserably startled. He said: "I wonder whether—"

"Your daughter doesn't know?"

"She doesn't know, Mr. Valcour."

"I see no reason why she should."

"That is good of you. Well, well, so here you are, my good girl."

Freda said to Valcour: "Isn't he stunning? I suppose you two think you've got a corner on sunlight."

"You'll get freckles," Barlowe said. "Red-heads do."

"This red-head doesn't. I'm coated with coconut oil and am guaranteed to brown but not burn. Have I interrupted a directors' meeting?"

"You are just in time, my dear child, for a little pre-luncheon third degree. Mr. Valcour is passionately interested in what people were doing last night around two o'clock. Personally, I have no alibi but my dreams."

Freda said: "Father's always thinking about his stomach. He's champing for the gong. Two o'clock? That was just before Mrs. Wiggins brought back Liddy, wasn't it?"

"Liddy," Barlowe explained, "is an impolite contraction for Miss Lidia Singlestar. And I sent this woman to Miss Ketcham's to learn manners!"

"I did learn manners. I've lots of manners. Liddy wants me to call her Liddy as it makes her feel less Louisa Alcott. My dreams are my alibi, too, Mr. Valcour."

"You were asleep, Miss Barlowe?"

She said: "I hope so. They consisted in riding down Third Avenue under the elevated tracks in a boat."

"Your dreams?"

"Yes."

"How is Miss Singlestar to-day?"

"She's quite all right to-day." Freda added, not unsavagely: "And in my opinion she was quite all right last night. I think it's disgraceful, this—this—this clucking business and shaking of heads as if she'd been seeing things. She did see things. She saw Waverly Hedglin's dead body sitting in that chair. That's exactly what she saw. From the way people have been soothing her you'd think they thought her mentally unfit." Her laugh was a little sharp. "I must say it's the calmest and most politely casual murder I've ever attended."

Barlowe looked worried. "You mustn't let it get on your nerves, Freda," he said. "Just take it easy. It will come out all right."

She said shortly: "You didn't sit up all night with Liddy."

"And there isn't any proof as yet that there has been a murder. Is there, Mr. Valcour?"

"None whatever."

Freda said: "Well, I don't know what you want. Mr. Hedglin is gone, Liddy sees his body, and his body vanishes." Her voice was exasperated. "And everybody knits."

Valcour smiled. "It must seem that way, Miss Barlowe."

"Look here, Freda," Barlowe said. "Mr. Valcour's doing all he can."

"I know. It's just my nature to be impatient, Mr. Valcour. I'm just irritated about Liddy, about no one believing her. Do you?"

"I believe that Miss Singlestar did see a man sitting in the chair who either was Waverly Hedglin or else was disguised to resemble him. In the latter instance I don't believe the man was dead."

Freda said: "I never thought of that. What a perfectly splendid idea! Weird." She turned it over in her mind. "Masquerade. To confuse the real facts, of course. But would it? I mean advantageously?"

"To the criminal?"

"Yes."

"I don't see how it could. Do you?"

Freda liked puzzles. "This is rather fun, Mr. Valcour." She was abruptly serious. "It's fun for us," she said. "It isn't any fun for Peter."

Barlowe said: "She's calling him Peter."

"I'm calling him Peter because it annoys him." Her voice was sharp. "He's scared of girls. He's scared of me."

"Then do you think it's nice?"

"What's nice?"

"To annoy him?"

Freda shrugged and said: "What else is there to do? I've looked all over the yacht and haven't seen even a quoit. Peter needs sympathy."

"Well, I don't see how he's going to get it by being irritated by being called Peter."

She said: "Have you never heard of a counter-irritant?"

"Certainly I have, but I've always understood that the counter-irritant shouldn't be greater than the original irritation."

"That man," Freda said to Valcour, "is my father. He's balancing me against a killed uncle. I'm not being vulgarly flip. I don't think that Peter cared very much for his uncle."

Valcour said: "What makes you think so?"

"I don't know. I just think so." Freda looked genuinely frightened. "You aren't being so conventional as to think he did it, Mr. Valcour, are you? I mean any stupid business about the dependent-and-impoverished-heir-murdering-his-rich-uncle-just-on-the-point-of-changing-his-will sort of thing?"

"I don't think much of Miss Ketcham's syntax," Barlowe said.

"Neither do I. You aren't thinking that, Mr. Valcour?"

Valcour smiled pleasantly. "I'm not thinking anything, Miss Barlowe."

"That means you're still open to thinking it," Freda said. "Why will people go by faces? Just because he's ugly."

"She calls him Peter and she says he's ugly. My God, Valcour, she's in love with him."

Freda said: "Suppose I am?"

"It's brazen. I call it brazen. The woman hasn't a shred of maidenly reserve."

"Well, it's stupid. Peter would never kill anyone." She added with complacent illogic: "If he did, they'd deserve it."

"You think there's a chance, Miss Barlowe, that his uncle might have deserved it?"

Freda said: "You're twisting my words. I didn't come up here for tricky questions, I came up to get some sunlight. I do wish you'd be reasonable, Mr. Valcour. About Peter."

Valcour laughed. "I am, Miss Barlowe; heaven knows I am. Nobody knows better than a policeman what hearts of gold may beat beneath a rough exterior."

"Who says he has a rough exterior?"

"I've often wondered," Barlowe said, "from which side of our family my daughter inherited her dash of hornet."

"You can see what I'm up against, Mr. Valcour. He's calling me a hornet. First it's a counterbalance to a killed uncle and now it's a hornet. In another minute he'll be accusing me of sharpening my serpent's tooth. I should have been born an orphan."

"It's a lucky thing, my good girl, that you weren't born twins."

"I suppose that's my cue for bursting into tears. Well, I won't. I'm going back downstairs and do some calling."

"Calling?"

Freda said, looking back at them as she moved away through the white hot sunlight: "Some calling Peter Peter."

Barlowe was serious again, a little empty, as if a lot of him had gone off with her, leaving him unfilled. "You can understand, Mr. Valcour," he said, "why I would go to rather great limits never to have her know."

"But doesn't it worry you, Mr. Barlowe?"

"The fact that Bettle knows? That you know?"

"Yes."

"Bettle's a queer man, Mr. Valcour, but he's straight. He has odd views, but he is absolutely sincere in them." Barlowe's curious and simple earnestness robbed his words of their extravagance. "I think," he said slowly, "that if Bettle were an engine and his wife were on the tracks in front of him, and the tracks led to the fulfillment of one of his views, he wouldn't stop. He'd keep on going and would crush her even if his own heart were crushed out, too. When he says a thing, he means it. He has said that he won't tell. I feel a good deal in that way about you, Mr. Valcour."

Valcour said quietly: "How about the people in Hedglin's office?"

"They know?"

"They know."

"I'm sorry." For a fat man, Barlowe looked very thin, very unfilled. "I'm sorry about that," he said.

CHAPTER TWENTY-ONE

A SYMBOL OF EVIL IS COLD

Miss Singlestar knew from her watch that luncheon was nearing and that she ought to be starting the process which was vaguely labeled by her as "freshening up." But it was so heavenly quiet and peaceful on the after-deck, on a wicker lounge, with the blue cup of sea lifting and sinking beyond the taffrail, while deck awning shaded her coolly from hot blinding sun.

Lethargically hypnotic were the waves, the sun-flash on their crests, the temperate air, and the confusing terrors of last night were drifting with the yacht's churned wake into dwindling streaks astern. How differently, she thought, things seemed in daytime!

She might have been mistaken. So many people had told her that she must have been. Not mistaken as to there having been a man in the chair, but as to his having been Waverly Hedglin, and as to his having been dead. She did hope it was so, and that that little drop had not been blood.

She smiled quite brightly at Valcour, who had just come along and who was sitting down on the lounge beside her. She said: "I've been thinking, Mr. Valcour, that I may have been mistaken."

"Because so many people have told you so?"

"Oh, do you think it's because of that?"

"It would naturally cause you to have some doubt."

"Doesn't it? They've been so very decided."

"Who has been, Miss Singlestar?"

"Well, that young Peter Moore boy for one. He doesn't seem ugly a bit after you've talked with him for a while, don't you think so?"

"People always look different after you get to know them."

"Don't they? It's as if the inside of them started coming out."

"Who else besides Peter, Miss Singlestar?"

"Almost everybody, Mr. Valcour. Even the stewardess said a word or so about it when she came up to do my cabin this morning. Mr. Bettle was the most insistent. He is so very positive that the man could not have been Mr. Hedglin. I do wish I knew. It's confusing to feel one may not know a thing one knows."

"Isn't it all a little clearer to you this morning? Looking back on it?"

"Certain things are. The curious part about it is that I can't concentrate on the man's face. The face is now quite vague."

"What things are clearer?"

"I think the man's hand is, and his arm. The way they moved."

Valcour said sharply: "Moved?"

"Yes. You see, the yacht was rolling rather badly and the man's arm slipped off the chair arm and slid down along the side. It did so oddly. I don't know just how to explain it, Mr. Valcour, but there was something a little *unpleasant* about the way it slid down along the side of the chair."

"It didn't just slump down, Miss Singlestar?"

"No, it was most unpleasant. It *slid* along. As if it were an effort."

Valcour thought: *Rigor mortis, attacking first the head and working downwards—reaching the arm—four, five, six hours after death, according to the conditions—death did not come as a shock, or the muscles would have bound and become set almost immediately—death was therefore unexpected and must have come unseen—an attack from behind?—an attack that must have occurred between, roughly, eight and ten o'clock—and Hedglin boarded the yacht at nine, and was seen leaving it about nine-thirty—if he did leave it.*—Valcour smiled pleasantly and said: "I'm sorry you are becoming undecided about the man's features, Miss Singlestar. Had you seen Mr. Hedglin frequently?"

"No, only once, Mr. Valcour. He was at the Bettle home when Mrs. Bettle invited Freda and me to join the cruise."

"Then if you weren't any more familiar with his features than that, there really is a chance that you may have been mistaken?"

"That is what they have been telling me. I *do* so hope it is so." Her watch was compelling. It was quite immutable, this law of hers about freshening up. She stood and said: "It's almost luncheon time. I'll have to run along and freshen up." She went over to the rail where arcing sunlight shot white splotches with shadows of blue and of hot siennas. "It's too lovely, Mr. Valcour. It's all too lovely to spoil with all of this. To mingle murder with the glory done to God."

Miss Singlestar moved off toward her freshening, and Valcour was thoughtful by the rail. *The glory done to God.* Copper stills were an odd offering to that glory. If the strange and bulky cargo were copper stills. If Miss Singlestar meant, as he thought she had meant, the stranger purpose of this cruise. It was hotly, whitely, close to noon. An hour, he decided, when most probably a fashionable practitioner could best be caught in his office. He wanted to call up Dr. Arthur Andrew. He wanted to ask Dr.

Andrew about Waverly Hedglin's state of health. He wanted to ask him especially about the condition of Waverly Hedglin's heart.

The boat deck was deserted, except forward on the bridge, where Valcour could see Captain Jorgensen and his two officers preparing to shoot the midday sun. He thought: *Everyone else is freshening up; what a balance wheel habit is!*

Valcour opened the wireless-room door and went inside. He stood near the doorway, watching, sensing an odd electric tension in the air, caught by Anthony Bettle's overpowering bigness which was a heavily charged cloud standing above young Meddletree. Meddletree was seated before the operating desk in a chair. Ebonite earphones were crisp black pools upon Meddletree's white skin, and above tight bloodless lips. Meddletree's dark eyes were astonishingly hot and angry.

"Come in, Mr. Valcour, and please close the door." Bettle's voice was impartial. It was cold. It was decisive with an unalterable finality. "There is no necessity for our broadcasting this unpleasant situation about the yacht."

"What situation, Mr. Bettle?" Valcour said.

Bettle pointed a finger toward the operating desk. Valcour saw the souvenir ashtray which "the girl" had brought back with her from her excursion to Atlantic City. For a minute he was confused. He had expected, from the tension, from young Meddletree's general bloodlessness, heaven knows what. Then he noticed it, crushed out and cold, lying in the ashtray. The cigarette.

It was momentarily absurd, the inconsequential childishness of it. Then he thought: *This is not absurd, or inconsequential, or childish in the least.* He remembered that nothing raised anger to such white and dangerous heat as a battle for one's beliefs. That crushed-out little thing in the ashtray wasn't a cigarette. It was a symbol. It was a massed and flaunting enemy in brazen attack against a belief. It was a hostile army hurled into the field by white-lipped young Meddletree against Anthony Bettle.

"This man is nuts, Mr. Valcour," Meddletree said.

Bettle grew deadly pale, and Valcour thought: *The argument must have gone pretty far.* Except in irreparably desperate extremities, wireless operators did not as a rule term yacht owners as "this man," or assert that they had gone nuts.

Bettle's voice was absolutely dispassionate. "There is a clause in the Articles, Mr. Valcour, which expressly binds the members of this ship's complement against the use of liquor or tobacco in any form for the duration of their service on board."

"*I didn't smoke the damn thing, I tell you. I don't know how it got there.*"

Bettle went on, ignoring Meddletree's sharp, almost hysterical tenseness entirely: "Any infringement of that rule amounts, in plain language, to insubordination on the high seas. Under maritime law that is a grave offense and can be drastically punished."

Valcour thought: *Bettle doesn't mean that. There are any number of maritime laws that he might find flouted and which wouldn't bother him a bit. He's taking this business as deliberate insubordination against himself, against his very sincere and honestly cherished pet belief.* Valcour said: "Perhaps Mr. Meddletree has some explanation?"

"*Talking to a stone, Mr. Valcour—that's what it is—talking to a damn pig-headed stone—*"

Valcour said rapidly: "I'm sure that you realize, Mr. Bettle, that this youngster has been deeply upset by the attack which he suffered last night. Under the circumstances, shouldn't one make allowances?" He wished, futilely, that young Meddletree would calm down. He knew that there was little more excessive than the limits of self-pity and of headless vilification to which an unimportant and financially poor employee would go when the floodgates of custom, of self-consciousness, of fear of discharge, were opened and all the bottled-up inhibitions against a wealthy, powerful, and irritating employer were loosed. They took it (these employees) as their moment. One step in itself being fatal, was their reasoning, why not go a mile?

Bettle was beautifully calm. "The explanation, Mr. Valcour, is very simple. Mr. Meddletree claims he had no knowledge that the cigarette was there."

"*It wasn't there, I tell you!*"

Bettle said: "But it is there, Mr. Meddletree."

Young Meddletree stood up, pushing the chair back violently. He took off the earphones and slammed them down on the desk. Valcour thought, for an instant, that he was going to hit Bettle.

"*You dirty, smug, self-satisfied, rich old fool—you, you lousy hypocrite, mouthing about God and rolling your fat old eyes up to heaven with a hold full of—*"

Bettle's fist was a pile driver, and young Meddletree sagged weakly, crumpled weakly, to the floor. Bettle stared down at him stupidly. "I shouldn't have done that," he said.

"No, Mr. Bettle, you should not have done that," said Valcour.

CHAPTER TWENTY-TWO

STRANGE PRESSURE PRESSES DRUMS

Young Meddletree's shouting (he had been yelling his epithets at the very top of his lungs) had drawn the bridge crowd from their computation of noonday observations and collected them at the wireless-room door, which Captain Jorgensen had opened. He had opened it in time for them to see the blow. He had become violently, instantly angry. "Dear man!" he had shouted at Bettle. "You cannot strike one of my men like that."

White and hot was the sunlight pouring over broad backs into the shadowed room. The bridge crowd looked, to Valcour, distinctly ugly. There was a close-knittedness about them, an immediate drawing together into a common front against an attack made by an outsider against one of them, against a man of the sea. Valcour said: "The provocation against Mr. Bettle was extreme, Captain Jorgensen."

"I am not apologizing," Bettle said. His voice was calm again, very strong and confident again. "I did not strike that blow. God, gentlemen, struck that blow."

They were astonished, profoundly so, into complete silence, into letting Bettle move through them and out onto the deck in this astonished silence, into watching Bettle move off through stillness and through hot white sun.

Mr. Jones shrugged faintly and nodded toward Meddletree. "We might as well stretch him on his bunk," he said. "If he gets slugged once more, he'll be out."

Captain Jorgensen was in a most unfamiliar state of being too bewildered for words. He hurried after Bettle and remembered, as he reached the ladder down which Bettle was just so serenely disappearing, to close his still-opened mouth.

Valcour watched Mr. Jones and Mr. Doorn lift young Meddletree and carry him through the connecting door into his quarters. Valcour went over to the operating desk and picked up the cigarette butt from the ashtray. It was a commonly smoked and well-known brand. He shrugged and dropped it back into the tray again. He went through the connecting door.

Meddletree had been liberally splashed with cold water. He was sitting on the edge of his bunk, quite fully recovered. He was very belligerent. "I'm going to sue him," he was saying. "I'll sue him for attack. You saw him hit me, Mr. Valcour? You saw I didn't raise a finger against him?"

Valcour said quietly: "You did call him some pretty strong things, Mr. Meddletree."

"He called me a liar. I didn't lie. I never saw that cigarette before in my life until he pointed his finger at it."

"How do you think that it got there?"

"I don't know how it got there. I don't give a good damn how it got there."

"Were you in the wireless room all morning?"

"No, I wasn't. I was on the bridge for quite a while until it was time to get the time signals at noon from Arlington."

"I see. Then practically anybody could have gone in and dropped that butt on the tray. Did you gentlemen see anyone about the wireless-room door?"

"I was doing some stuff in the charthouse," Doorn said.

Mr. Jones was thoughtful. "I did see Mr. Barlowe near it at some time or other."

"Shortly before noon?"

"Yes, Mr. Valcour. It must have been just before noon."

"Did you see him actually entering or leaving the wireless room?"

"You're right. I did."

"Which?"

"Leaving it. Then he went down the ladder amidships to the main deck."

Meddletree had worked himself into a full rage again.

"You see? Barlowe left that butt there. I'll teach that lousy smug slob to call me a liar!"

"I'm not belittling the unfortunate blow Mr. Bettle gave you," Valcour said, "but there is a difference between calling a man a liar and in saying that you don't believe a thing."

"He had no right to hit me."

"Not a bit."

"I'll sue him. I've got witnesses." Meddletree was almost at the top of his lungs again. "He like to bust my jaw. I bet he broke a bone or something. I bet I'll be laid up for weeks."

"Take it easy, Sparks," Mr. Jones said. "What's a crack?"

"You'd know what it was soon enough if you'd got this one."

Mr. Jones said: "I've got lots of cracks. How about snapping out of it and getting busy on the noon weather report? The Old Man's worried about the weather."

"Well, I'm not."

Mr. Doorn said heavily: "Well, you damn well soon may be."

"I'm injured, and I'm going to sue." Meddletree's eyes looked deliberately calculating. "My whole jaw hurts. It's swelling up. I think I got a bone broken."

"Well, your tongue isn't broken," Mr. Jones said. "Get busy on that weather report, will you?"   Young Meddletree groaned realistically and lay back upon the pillows. Valcour could sense the palpable shift in attitude of the two officers, in their sympathy, in a slow erasing of it. Meddletree could sue Bettle as much as he pleased and they would be glad to back him up. But malingering was unfavorably looked upon at sea. There was no opportunity, as there was on land, to replace the malingerer.

Meddletree said: "I won't." He opened his eyes and added hastily, before closing them again: "I would if I could, but I can't. You guys will remember that I said that."

Doorn muttered something forcefully nasty, and Mr. Jones said: "Well, ships did totter along for a good many years without the aids and blessings of wireless. And its operators. I guess we can manage to keep afloat for the next couple of days." He shrugged and said, as he followed Valcour and Doorn through the connecting door: "I hope that when the Old Man starts nursing you, you will enjoy your convalescence."

They stood for a moment on deck, Valcour and young Jones and the sour-looking Mr. Doorn. Valcour said: "I am intensely stupid about the weather. All New Yorkers are. Our sky is simply disconnected slices that we don't even bother to ignore. To-day looks perfect to me—clear sky, strong sun, windless, and hot. Mr. Bettle is worried about it. Captain Jorgensen is. You two gentlemen are. What's wrong?"

"The glass is wrong," Mr. Doorn said sourly.

Valcour smiled. "That still leaves me in the condition of a would-be intelligent child."

Mr. Jones explained: "The barometer is going in for some tumbles, Mr. Valcour. So far as the sky is concerned there is nothing to get alarmed about. It may be just a local atmospheric depression." He gestured vaguely at cupped horizons. "Odd things often happen in this area and during this season of the year." He said again: "Not a thing to be alarmed about."

Valcour felt they were consciously keeping something from him, some secret and instinctive knowledge which was inbred with men who live at sea. He said: "What do you think of Mr. Meddletree? Do you think he'll stick to his determination?"

Doorn said: "He'll stick." He added a few pointed and doubtlessly inaccurate genealogical remarks. "He'll nurse that jaw until we hit port."

"No more wireless, then? Isn't there anyone else who can operate the sets?"

Doorn said: "No." His expression implied that he wouldn't be caught dead with one of the contraptions.

Mr. Jones was vague. "I think that in an emergency Captain Jorgensen might be most persuasive." He started to drift forward. "I've got to finish my calculations. I suppose we'll have some more of that lovely lousy suet pudding for lunch."

Doorn stood looking speculatively at Valcour for a moment, looking at him heavily with his sullen, soured eyes. "A man is a fool to sneer at the old saying," he said.

"What old saying are you thinking of, Mr. Doorn?"

Doorn started after Mr. Jones. His voice came back to Valcour: "The curse of wealth."

And that, thought Valcour, was all as it might be, but what of it? He was intensely concerned about the whole cigarette business. Had Barlowe dropped it in the tray? Barlowe had the intelligence to, the intelligence to see precisely what would be the results. He had the incentive to prevent any further messages from Hedglin's office, messages which might fall directly into Meddletree's hands for delivery, and so get about. Get about until they got to Freda. Barlowe would do a lot to stop his past from getting to Freda. There was this possible marriage business between young John Bettle and Freda. Would Bettle let that go through knowing, as Barlowe claimed Bettle knew, that Barlowe was George Sincere? But was anything more astonishing than that Bettle, with his views, should willfully have in his employ the man who had been George Sincere? *Somebody*, thought Valcour, *is crossing the ice, and it isn't little Eva.* His head, which had subconsciously been bothering him all morning, began to feel definitely uncomfortable. He could feel a slight but noticeable pressure on his ear drums.

Burke was coming along the deck toward him. "The lunch gong struck five minutes ago, sir," Burke said. "Sorry to interrupt your thinking." Valcour walked back with Burke toward the ladder. "You haven't interrupted me," he said. "Lunch will be a relief. My head has been feeling funny all morning."

"Funny, sir?"

"Yes. It feels just now as if something were pressing on my ear drums."

Burke stopped dead in his tracks, and Valcour thought he paled a little. Burke said: "I can feel it in my ears, too."

"What do you suppose it is?"

Burke said: "Most likely it's the humidity. Most likely the humidity's quite high, Mr. Valcour." He seemed to be thinking of something, trying to remember something. "Nothing to bother about."

"Then why do you think there is?"

Burke started for the ladder again, and permitted Valcour to precede him down it. "Sailors have a lot of woman in them," he said, when they had reached the main deck. "With their old wives' tales."

Valcour stared at Burke searchingly, at Burke's definite paleness, at the conscious vagueness in his eyes. "What's this one?" he said.

"Just the pressure, sir."

"On our ear drums?"

"Yes, Mr. Valcour. Things happen sometimes, I've heard it said. When there's pressure on the ear drums. The rest of the party are all in the dining saloon, sir."

"Thank you, Burke."

"Yes, sir."

CHAPTER TWENTY-THREE

THE SURFACE IS A PLACID SEA

The dining saloon of the *Crusader* was just forward of the saloon, on the starboard side. Its walls were veneered with applewood panels highly waxed, and its simple effective decor must have cost, Valcour thought, a fortune. He took his place at the left of Helen Bettle, who was at one end of the table. He said: "I didn't hear the gong."

Helen smiled and said placidly: "I've always wanted a bugle. You can hear them so much better than gongs at sea. Anthony doesn't like bugles. That bouillon is scaldingly hot, Mr. Valcour. He says they startle him. It should have been cold." She turned to Barlowe, who was at her right. "Don't you think it's hot enough to have the bouillon cold?"

Barlowe said: "I am always in doubt. Jellying it sometimes robs it of its flavor. What a good chef you have!"

Helen said vaguely: "Yes, isn't he?" and turned her eyes carefully toward Freda, who was beside Valcour, between Valcour and John. John had said to her when she had arranged the seating that he was going to sit beside Freda. And there he was. Sitting beside Freda and not, Helen thought, looking especially happy about it.

"He is a Frenchman," Helen went on automatically to Barlowe, "and that is all I know about him. Wharton says that with a chef it's enough." John wasn't paying a bit of attention to Freda. He was staring across the table at Peter Moore, who was sitting between Mr. Barlowe and Wharton. It was Peter who was paying attention to Freda, talking with her right across the table—talking back at her, that is, when he had to. Peter looked flushed and sick about something. The way people look when they're worrying dreadfully about something. Something for which they can't find any healing remedy. Freda was really doing all of the talking. Calling him Peter. (Freda was saying to him: "Freda isn't the sort of name that bites you. You can say it, Peter dear, with perfect impunity. F is for her face with candor shining, R is for the red that's in her hair, E stands for her eyes with…") John was looking angry. Helen could always tell at once when John was angry. Even when John was quite a small boy that little scar on his temple would redden. Thinking he could fly. How stunned his face had been, when they'd picked him up! When Anthony and she, with such fright in their hearts, had picked him up. Such fat little legs… "Yes, Mr. Valcour, it has been somewhat oppressive to-day. My ears have felt uncomfortable."

"A pressure against the drums, Mrs. Bettle?"

Helen repeated tranquilly: "Yes, a pressure against the drums." Freda *was* pretty. With that striking red hair. How careful you had to be, Helen thought, with red hair! Real violet-looking eyes. And any girl who went to Miss Ketcham's was automatically "nice." Why *had* Carlotta said that Freda's mother was a pickpocket? It was such palpable nonsense. Miss Ketcham's. Helen dabbled for a speculative moment with kleptomania. Was it inheritable? Some of the best people… "Why should it be the humidity, Mr. Valcour? I always thought that humidity made you wet. What was that, Anthony dear?" Anthony had been listening to her from the other end of the table, where he was sitting with Carlotta at his right and Miss Singlestar at his left. "It doesn't make you wet?" Helen turned again to Valcour. "Anthony says it doesn't make you wet. Miss Singlestar would be a very pretty woman if she arranged her hair less simply."

Valcour looked at Helen Bettle's own hair, at the collapsed-pompadour look about it. He thought: *She too could be a pretty woman.* Helen had turned again to Barlowe, and Valcour was listening to John's voice, coming sideways across Freda's baiting of Peter. John was saying: "That's off. That's definitely off."

John was saying this to Carlotta, saying it harshly, with finality, and very irritable about it. Valcour wondered what was off and why.

Then Carlotta was speaking: "Perhaps later, John. It is, remember, for your good."

Carlotta was keeping her temper, Valcour decided, just barely. Her voice had an edge to it. And John said to her: "I don't believe in that truck, I tell you."

Bettle said to John loudly, sharply: "Don't speak like that!" and conversation around the table dribbled, died into stillness, a stillness in which John's mumbled "I'm sorry, Carlotta," was very plain.

"Sauces, Mr. Barlowe," Helen said placidly, "are almost all of them built upon a foundation of melted butter, and with so many good bottled condiments nowadays to choose from, if you simply use melted butter for a base…"

"It isn't what you say, Peter, it's what you don't…"

Wharton said: "An amber-jack, my dear Miss Singlestar, is a second-string tarpon. Amber-jacks act as substitutes in the Florida waters while the tarpon, quite sensibly, go south for the winter. I recall one day of liquid sunshine, which is Florida's term for the phenomenon we call rain, when…"

Talk swelled again and Burke, with his assistant, removed dishes, added new ones, and Valcour heard Freda say to John with suspicious sweetness: "But of course, John. I'd love it. At three? Oh, dear—I believe Peter is teaching me quoits at three. He's going to weave some out of bits of rope. You are, Peter, aren't you?"

Peter said: "I could teach you quoits!"

And Valcour was impressed with the almost studied care with which none of them made any reference to what must have been so compellingly on their minds: Hedglin. The complete inexplicableness of Hedglin. Helen Bettle was saying to him: "…such a pity. Anthony is so easily upset, Mr. Valcour."

Valcour was confused. He had lost the beginning. He said: "I beg your pardon, Mrs. Bettle?"

"I say that that business about the wireless man is such a pity, Mr. Valcour. Anthony is so easily upset. Wharton says that every stolid business man is a *diva* at heart."

Bettle said to Helen from the other end of the table: "Wharton enjoys being mistaken."

"My dear Anthony," Wharton said, "for once you find me speechless. If I know anything about wireless operators, which I don't, I would take steps. There is no advice so pregnant with meaning, or so utterly incomprehensible, as to tell a person that he ought to take steps."

It interested Valcour, the seizing of everyone so avidly upon this side issue to the main problem. It was as close, it seemed, as they cared to come to the business about Hedglin. He said: "Mr. Meddletree seems to be in for a course of malingering. The first officer believes that the set will be closed down until we reach port and can replace him."

Bettle said: "Nonsense."

"Mr. Meddletree strikes me as being a tenaciously stubborn young man."

"Mr. Meddletree, Mr. Valcour, is inconsequential."

Barlowe said: "There is a substitute wireless man in the crew?"

"No," Bettle said. "My son."

Valcour stared steadily at Barlowe, carefully observant, while Barlowe said casually: "John knows wireless?"

"John," Bettle said, "was a wireless operator on a merchant vessel for one year. I chartered it for that purpose. It was my intention that in that fashion John might come into intimate contact with humanity and with the world. It was essential for him to have some first-hand knowledge of men if he is to carry on my work."

Barlowe's voice had an unnatural quality. Even Freda noticed it, and she stared at her father, puzzled.

"I didn't know that," Barlowe said. "I didn't know."

CHAPTER TWENTY-FOUR

LIPS SMILE WITHOUT EYES

"Dr. Andrew? This is Lieutenant Valcour, of the New York police force. I am talking from Mr. Anthony Bettle's yacht, the *Crusader*. I suppose that the newspapers have given you information as to Mr. Waverly Hedglin's disappearance?"

Dr. Andrew's voice was noticeably interested. "They have, Lieutenant. Extraordinary! You have news?"

"Unfortunately none, Doctor. Mr. Hedglin was a patient of yours, I understand?"

"Yes, I've treated him for the past ten years or so."

"Then perhaps you will be good enough to tell me something about his general state of health? You see, Doctor, the police are anxious to know every angle. There is a possibility that some shock may have influenced his mind or his heart."

"His mind, my dear sir, is absolutely sound. His general condition is almost perfect. His heart, however, is questionable. Shall I go into technical details?"

"I'm afraid I wouldn't be able to grasp them, Doctor. If you could just give me a general idea?"

"Simply a weakish heart then, Lieutenant. Not in the sense that Mr. Hedglin had to exercise great care—the ordinary habits of living would not bother him a bit—but I have advised him seriously against any excessive or sudden strain."

Valcour said carefully: "Would the condition of his heart affect the proportionate strength of, say, a blow or a wound in order to make either fatal? I mean would a lesser blow or wound prove fatal than would ordinarily be required if his heart were in first-class condition?"

"Oh, yes. By all means, yes. Even a moderately struck blow in the region of the cardiac muscles or on the brain, near any of the nerve centers—But my dear Lieutenant, has there been? You do know something definite? The newspapers have been so confusing, so contradictory. Hedglin has been seen in a thousand places, he's alive, he's dead, he has been drowned, he has absconded to South America—heaven knows with or from what—really—"

"No, Doctor, nothing definite is known at all. It was good of you to give me the information. I hope I haven't disturbed you."

"Not at all, Lieutenant. I am enormously interested. Couldn't I keep in touch?"

"I'm sure that the commissioner will be glad to keep you advised, if you phone him occasionally."

"That's right. You are on a yacht. Most interesting. Most."

"Thank you again, Doctor. Good-bye."

"Not at all. No trouble at all. Good-bye." Valcour replaced the receiver. He said to John, who was seated at the operating desk opening switches: "I think I had better say the same thing to you that I did to Mr. Meddletree."

"What's that, Mr. Valcour?"

Valcour smiled agreeably. "I'd be generally careful. Things happened to young Meddletree. I don't want them to happen to you. Carry a gun with you, if you have one. If you haven't, I'll see whether any of the officers has one and will borrow it for you. Bolt your door at night, and stick around with people. Try not to be alone any more than you can help it, especially in any out-of-the-way places on the yacht. Don't go wandering off with any single person—make it a threesome, or a foursome if you can. Be careful about eating things at odd hours, drinking things. This sounds very melodramatic, doesn't it? But you can't say things like this without sounding melodramatic. And they have to be said."

John finished with switches. He looked a little pale. He said: "This blow or wound business, Mr. Valcour, that you were talking about with the doctor—what made you say that?"

"I am working with hypotheses until we have a few real facts to go ahead on. How about messages coming for the yacht? Are you going to listen-in, or get in touch with shore every so often? How are you going to work it?"

"You're expecting one, Mr. Valcour?"

"I am. Quite an important one."

"Concerning Mr. Hedglin?"

"Concerning Mr. Hedglin's briefcase." Valcour smiled amiably. "You must forgive me for not being more explicit. I am myself still in a state of being thoroughly bewildered."

John said slowly: "I don't believe you, Mr. Valcour."

"Why on earth do you say that?"

"I think you know a lot of things about this business. I think you know lots."

"What, for example?"

"I think you believe Miss Singlestar's story about the man in the chair being Mr. Hedglin's body, and the spot on the back of the chair being a drop of blood. I think you believe that the body was thrown over the side by the killer."

Valcour said: "And you? Do you believe these things, too?"

John looked very worried, very young. He seemed tired, physically, spiritually tired about something, almost washed out. "Of course I believe them, Mr. Valcour. We all do, really. We've got it in the back of our heads all the time." He added uncertainly: "It isn't nice. Having things like that—ideas—in the back of your head. I think we're all of us afraid to admit the fact that we have them there even to ourselves."

"Why are you so sure that I believe them?"

"You wouldn't have spoken to the doctor the way you did if you didn't, Mr. Valcour. You wouldn't have been so careful about having that carafe-ful of tap water and the wicker you cut from the chair put in the captain's safe if you didn't believe all those things. Would you?"

"After all, that was simply taking routine precautions."

John sighed. He seemed older-looking, more weary-looking. "All right," he said. "I'll get in touch with the shore stations every hour, Mr. Valcour, until your message comes through. Are you expecting it around any definite hour?"

"I'm not. It may come through this afternoon, or it may not come through until to-morrow. Perhaps not even then."

John said suddenly, uncomfortably: "I hope you aren't putting any stock in this stuff about Freda's mother."

"How did Miss Balfé happen to speak about it?"

"You've heard about Maybelle, Mr. Valcour?"

"Yes, from your father."

"Well, it was Maybelle who told Carlotta in one of her messages that Freda's mother was a pickpocket."

They both heard the deck door to the wireless room opening, and turned to see Horatio Barlowe stepping across its combing. Barlowe's smile was mechanically genial. "Our new operator, I see," he said.

Valcour looked thoughtfully at the room's ports. One of them was open.

John flushed and said: "Did you hear what I just said, Mr. Barlowe?"

"No. Should I have?"

"I'm glad you didn't. It was just some nasty nonsense."

Barlowe's laugh was deep and soft and hearty; it did not set well with the delicate and unusual paleness of his skin, and his eyes in their jovial creases were undisguisedly cruel and hard. "I don't believe in eavesdropping," he said. "In nine times out of ten whatever you hear is unpleasant. And ten times out of ten it's true."

"We weren't talking about you, Mr. Barlowe." John added hurriedly: "Can I put a call through for you?"

The deck door swung open again, violently, suddenly, and Captain Jorgensen was standing there, looking at young John Bettle, saying: "Hah! That is good. So you can operate it. You must be quick, man. You must get me a weather report at once."

Barlowe said: "Some trouble brewing, Captain?"

"I do not know, Mr. Barlowe. I cannot tell what it is we must expect. I do not like it. I think that some real hard weather is due to commence.

As you can feel, we are beginning to lollop foolishly on a swell which is bigger getting, and which has no precision about it. It is coming at us from all points at once."

John started tuning in again, while Valcour and Barlowe gathered with Captain Jorgensen just outside the open wireless-room door.

"It is hard for me to reconcile the fact that the sky is so clear," Valcour said.

Captain Jorgensen was impatient. "The sky has nothing to do with it, man. The glass is doing stupid and foolish tumblings. She is almost down to twenty-nine point thirty. Then I shall ask you, gentlemen, to look at the water."

They looked, Valcour and Barlowe, at the water, at the criss-cross swelling sea, smooth and blue and warm beneath a clear blue sun-hot sky.

"Of course I can feel the motion," Barlowe said, "but it's pretty smooth-looking water to me. I can't see anything funny about it."

Captain Jorgensen gave it up. He said with disturbing quietness: "That is what is funny about it. There is not a whitecap on the whole surface of that sea."

CHAPTER TWENTY-FIVE

MR. BURKE IS DEEPLY ANNOYED

Mr. Burke was receiving. He was seated at his desk in his quarters. They were (the steward's quarters) below-decks, on the starboard side, and well forward of amidships. Lined up in a row before him were the three men in his department: the chef, the messboy, and the pantryman. Burke's somberly dark eyes stared out at them from his pallid face. "I will thank you lobsters," he said, "to tell me which one of you took it."

The chef, whose command of English was restricted almost to the point of being negligible, scowled darkly and said: "We 'ave no lobstair."

Burke said irritably: "I know we haven't. I'm not speaking about lobsters. I'm speaking to them. I want to know who took it."

The chef's shrug was dislocating. "'Ow can we take 'im if we 'ave no lobstair?" He was getting good and mad. He didn't like being yanked out of bed from his afternoon nap for a chat about lobsters.

The pantryman explained: "He ain't asking you for lobsters, Frenchy. He's calling you one."

"Me? 'E name me a lobstair?"

"Sure. Just now we're all lobsters. He wants to know who took it?"

The messboy said earnestly: "I didn't. What would I want it for?"

"You would want it," Burke said severely, "for your pants."

"'E, zis man, 'e name me a lobstair?"

"Well, *I* didn't take it," the pantryman said. "What's the big row about anyway, Mr. Burke? Was it stuffed with diamonds?"

Mr. Burke continued severe. "It was not stuffed with diamonds, but it's the only one on the ship and I want it back at once. Who's got it?"

"Well, I ain't," the pantryman repeated, "and Oscar here says he ain't, so it must be Frenchy. Maybe he wanted it for his beard. How about it, Frenchy, did you want it for your beard?"

"Are you good and crazee? I 'ave a lobstair for my beard? To 'ell wiz you." The chef turned abruptly and flung the door angrily open. He found his not unmagnificent exit momentarily blocked. He glared for a second at Valcour. He said: "*Pardon, monsieur!*"   Valcour came inside. "Am I interrupting something?" he said.

Burke stood up. "Not at all, Mr. Valcour. You bugs clear out. I'll get after you again later."

The pantryman and messboy followed the chef out, and Valcour said: "Trouble, Mr. Burke?"

"Just a little, sir. Nothing to bother about. Won't you sit down?"

"Thank you. Nice quarters you've got here."

"They're not bad."

"I just want to check over a few points with you." Valcour steadied himself by gripping the arms of the chair. "Quite a lot of motion, isn't there."

"It is a bit roughish, sir. We'll need the racks for dinner. What was it you wished to check up?"

"When the different people came on board. You stayed on deck most of the time during the evening we sailed, didn't you?"

"On deck or thereabouts. On the bridge for a while. But I kept an eye on things."

"Then see if I have this straight: Mr. and Mrs. Bettle, John Bettle, Wharton Luke, and Carlotta Balfé boarded the yacht first?"

"Yes, sir. They dined on board."

"Then Mr. Barlowe arrived around eight?"

"Yes, about eight."

"Mr. Hedglin and Peter Moore about nine?"

"Just at nine, Mr. Valcour. I heard two bells as they came over the side."

"And Miss Barlowe and Miss Singlestar did not get here until around ten-thirty?"

"Just about. A few minutes after, if anything."

"Were you in the cabins much? Or in the passage that runs between them?"

"Only when racking bags, Mr. Valcour. I was on deck mostly, or on the bridge. I had it on my mind."

"Had what, Mr. Burke?"

"Lithia water." Burke added earnestly: "There are moments when I thank God for all this sad affair about Mr. Hedglin. It keeps Mr. Luke from thinking."

"Were you in the passage at all between nine and nine-thirty?"

"Not after racking Mr. Moore's and Mr. Hedglin's stuff. I went out and up on the bridge again. I wasn't thinking of much else around then except would it get here. Have you noticed the face he makes at table, Mr. Valcour?"

"Mr. Luke?"

"Yes. Every time he reaches for his glass it's like a serpent had stung him. He's sticking to tea. Runs me ragged bringing him iced tea. Tea, he says, makes him less sick. He can't be drinking it all or he'd bust. I think he pours it down the sink."

"Mr. Burke, what was the trouble you were having just now? Do you mind telling me?"

"Not a bit. Somebody stole it and I want it back. It's the only one on the ship and I need it."

"What is?"

"My electric iron."

Valcour thought about this for a moment. "You believe somebody stole it?"

"Yes."

"Why? Don't you let people use it?"

"That's just it, Mr. Valcour. I never objected to anyone using it. Why should they steal it?"

"When did you miss it?"

"I didn't want it until about half an hour ago. It's kept over there in that locker. I know it was there when we sailed, but it ain't there now. I always check up on my things before we sail. I've got some pressing to do for Mr. Bettle, and with this rolling coming up I don't want flatirons bouncing all over the galley."

"Perhaps someone took it, broke it, and was afraid to bring it back."

"Do you think that's it?"

Valcour's voice was grave. He said: "I hope, Mr. Burke, that that is it."

CHAPTER TWENTY-SIX

THERE WAS A POOL AND SALT

By three o'clock the air was almost unbreathable and the pressure against his ear drums, instead of ceasing, had become noticeably stronger. Valcour walked toward the after-deck, balancing himself as well as he could against the uneasy motion of the yacht. He knew that Captain Jorgensen was secretly a very worried man.

The weather report which John had succeeded in getting had been disconcerting. It had contained no storm warnings. Its general forecast had been clement and in no respect different from any ordinary report for fair weather. In spite of it, in spite of clear blue skies, the glass had fallen lower still and the swell was increasing with its queer criss-cross, having none of the orderly quality of the normal swell which mounts in advance of a gale. Captain Jorgensen had said with his voice that it must be just a local atmospheric depression, but his worried eyes had said any number of different things.

Valcour found Carlotta alone on the after-deck, sitting on the wicker settee. He thought her huddled-looking. She was pressed against the wicker almost as if it were affording her some strange defense against a strange and unseen foe. It shocked him to see that her face was entirely clear of make-up. It gave her easily an added ten years. He said: "May I join you?"

Carlotta relaxed as he sat on the settee beside her. It was as if he had taken over part of the duties of its odd defense. She said: "It's true, Mr. Valcour. If you play with it long enough, it burns you."

"Fire?"

Carlotta shrugged impatiently. "Anything."

She seemed very miserable, a little astonished, and (Valcour thought) completely scared. He said: "Even spiritualism?"

"That is the only thing I have ever played with."

"Then it has been play?"

Her fingers were quite tight about his arm. "Mr. Valcour, I've had a few lucky breaks but they've all been *breaks*. You know what I mean?

I've got onto a few things here and there and used them at the right moment. You know the racket, you know how it's worked, don't you, Mr. Valcour?"

Her eagerness had a feverish note in it, her intense eagerness that he reassure her as to the mechanics in ordinary usage by fake mediums. He said: "I know the game."

"You know there's nothing in it? Nothing real? You know how it is?"

He said again, quietly, in face of this sudden and burning eagerness: "I know."

"Never, never once, Mr. Valcour, have I been inspired. Listen, let me tell you: my mother was an Armenian Jewess. She was funny, my mother. She made her living by telling fortunes in our room down on Hester Street. You could not breathe well in that room, or see it. You couldn't move a foot in it, Mr. Valcour, unless you stumbled over something. She would sit in it, my mother, and tell fortunes. All day long and into night our people would come to her and she would tell fortunes. They came," (her voice was as tight as the grip of her fingers on his arm), "because she told good fortunes, and things she told our people about would come true."

"What sort of things, Miss Balfé?"

Carlotta said impatiently: "No, no, I do not mean things like that, such as you mean. You are thinking of the 'strange dark man with money,' of the 'letter from across water'—no, not things like that. They would be real things, Mr. Valcour. Real things of life that people live with." Her voice weakened suddenly. She said: "That people die with."

"You feel that your mother was genuinely psychic?"

"She said she was not. She would laugh about it when she was alone with me in that thick-filled room—never once were the shades up in it, Mr. Valcour—she would tell me it was all a trick."

"And was it?"

"My mother-died before she could tell me just what was that trick."

"Then you drifted into spiritualism more or less naturally, Miss Balfé?"

"I got out. I got straight out of that room. But I never left it, Mr. Valcour. Always along with me, always right here, right inside of me here, is staying something of that room. I am smart. I am a rich woman. I live expensively. But I cannot cut it out of me. Either my mother or that room." Carlotta leaned very close to Valcour. She said: "Last night I was back in it again. Last night I was back there with my mother in that room."

He stared at her thoughtfully, gauging her cleverness, her smartness. He thought: *She isn't being clever or smart; she's being real. She's had a good sound fright*. He said: "Mr. Bettle told me something about it."

"Yes, I know. He doesn't believe it."

"Do you?"

Carlotta was being shrill. "How can I? What can I? I am not ignorant of self-hypnosis. I know very well that all last night I was upset."

He said: "Upset about what?"

Her fingers relaxed their grip. He could sense an immediate drawing-away from him, not physically, but as if Carlotta had stepped swiftly behind an obscuring wall. Her voice took on a touch of its normally affected tone. She said: "It was natural for all of us to be upset about Mr. Hedglin." She closed the sentence as if she were tying a neat knot, and sat there waiting; almost like a boxer she sat there in her corner of the wicker settee, waiting for Valcour to say something.

"Why," he said, "did you change the water in the carafe?"

Nothing moved about her, only her fingers which were briefly, tightly clenched and then were loose again. Her bloodless, paintless lips stayed closed. She sat like a not untragic stone while her eyes were restless about the deck.

He said: "You did change it, didn't you?"

Carlotta's smile was bewildering; there was an almost childish relief in it. "I will swear, Mr. Valcour, on any sacred thing which you may suggest, that I did not change the water in that carafe."

There was, he felt, a very definite catch in it somewhere. "Do you wish anyone to stand guard over you to-night?" he said.

It didn't shock her. It didn't, as he had hoped, swing her back into that puddle of foggy fear from which the business about Hedglin had lifted her. Carlotta's eyes were disturbingly mocking. She said: "Against what, Mr. Valcour?"

He controlled his rising impatience. "Against a possible fulfillment of your last night's premonition, Miss Balfé."

"What guard can there be against death?"

His voice was irritable. "Any number of reasonable precautions can be taken. As the most concrete example, I could stand at your door with a gun, if you liked."

Carlotta was genuinely puzzled. "To shoot *death*?"

He said : "To shoot whoever comes to kill you."

She was pressed back again against the wicker, with utterly bloodless skin, and her face was bewildered. "It wasn't that, Mr. Valcour. It wasn't that…"

He said sharply: "You must be explicit."

"It wasn't to be murder…"

The idea had shaken her profoundly, beaten her back into being huddled, weak. He said: "You must forgive my stupidity. Policemen are obsessed with homicide. You mustn't let my stupidness affect you."

"Is it?"

"I beg your pardon?"

"Is it stupidness?" She was in fog, and her voice was a weak thing feeling after something blindly.

"Tell me," he said gently, "what you know of the carafe."

"The water in it?"

"Yes?"

"The water in it was a pool—and salt…"

CHAPTER TWENTY-SEVEN

SLENDER FINGERS ARE BLACK STEEL

The sun was a red wet balloon puddling out beneath the sea's sharp western lip. There was nothing unusual in the splendid, lucent colors of the sunset sky. Thin and low in the distant west were three slender fingers of cold black steel. Valcour thought: *They are like bars imprisoning something which would spread danger if it were to escape.*

He kept a firm grip on the starboard rail, feeling a sense of exhilaration in the yacht's queer awkward lunging, the upward heaving rising against a clinging suction, up, and up, and up on a confusing crest, the freeing shudder of the engines, of the ship, as the propeller momentarily raced clear, then sinking, swiftly plunging, sinking into cross and sodden troughs molten with colors of the sky.

Burke was angling his way toward him. Burke said: "Dinner's ready, Mr. Valcour. If you want any."

Valcour smiled. "I think I could manage some. Rough, isn't it?"

"I'll say it's rough. The Old Man's fit to be tied."

"I shouldn't think it would be rough enough for that."

"It ain't the roughness that's bothering him." They started to make their way toward the saloon door. Burke said: "It's the glass that's bothering him. You won't have much company for dinner, Mr. Valcour."

"The motion's got the better of them?"

"They're in their cabins flat on their backs." Burke clutched a stanchion and added with resignation: "You might know he wouldn't be."

"There's a survivor?"

"Mr. Luke."

"How about the youngsters?"

"Young Mr. Bettle's up above in the wireless shack. He's getting down a message. There's been trouble, he says,"

"Trouble?"

"Trouble with the set; the speaking part of it."

"The telephone?"

"Yes. He says the static's fierce. He says all you can hear is dishpans. He's been working now for over an hour trying to get the message by straight wireless. He knows Morse code."

"Do you know whom it's for?"

"It's for you. He said not to bother you. He'll bring it down when it comes through."

They were at the saloon door. Burke opened it, and they went inside.

"Is he alone in the wireless room?" Valcour said.

"No, sir. Mr. Doorn is with him. He asked Mr. Doorn to stay in there with him."

"I see."

They went into the dining saloon. Wharton, very immaculate and unruffled, was alone at the table.

"I've never been in the hanging gardens of Shanghai," Wharton said, "but if they swing I imagine they must be something like this. The pepper has passed me five times. Don't sit across table from me, my dear Valcour, or we'll blend."

Valcour seated himself at Wharton's left. "I must be lined with cast iron," he said.

"They tell me that the seat of seasickness is in the head. You'd better retract the lining."

"I shall. I do."

"Steward, the tea is cold. Even if I could catch it, which I can't, it would be cold. You'll find it exhausted against the rack in that farther corner. Really, Valcour, the only civilized method for dining at sea is from funnels."

"I'll fetch some fresh tea at once, sir."

"Do."

Valcour steadied a plate of hors d'oeuvres with his hand. "You have to clutch it," he said. "I hope that the bulk of this dinner is solid."

"Will you join me in a sporting chance on the soup?"

"Gladly"

"Steward, I've changed that odd area which it pleases me to call my mind. I will have soup."

"Very good, sir."

Burke left the dining saloon.

"Tell me, my dear Valcour, what you think of that astonishing little explosion of Carlotta's."

"You know about it?"

"Oh, Anthony always tells me things I want to know. He tells them to me in desperation. He thinks it's the only way to get rid of me."

"What are your own reactions to it, Mr. Luke?"

"They're perfectly charming. Well, here it is again!" He caught the pepper. "I think she's frightened. Carlotta's so accustomed to frightening other people that it has stunned her. It has put her closer to being in a trance than she has ever before been in her life."

"She didn't connect homicide with it."

"Didn't she? That's odd. I did at once."

"I did, too. The idea shocked her. Really shocked her."

Wharton said carefully: "I wonder whether she's going in for any arrangements."

"I don't believe she is."

"Not that it matters. Nobody could possibly kill anyone on a night like this. Not even a bullet could follow a straight line. You'll forgive me for being untechnical in my trajectories?" Wharton stared in fascination at Burke, who had just come in. "The steward," he said, "is about to go back for more soup."

Burke muttered something as he picked himself up from the floor, and china clattered brokenly on a tray as he went out.

"The sea's acting up," Valcour said. "I wonder what's ahead of us."

"To be nautical, I think we're in for a good slant of dirty weather. The bridge crowd is running around masked like a lot of silly Pollyannas if anyone comes near them. This business about a local atmospheric depression is stupid. They know perfectly well it's a hurricane."

The word had a flat sound, like a lid on a pot in which some mess was boiling.

"Ever experienced a hurricane, Mr. Luke?"

"Never. I imagine they're salutary."

"For the ego?"

"Exactly. For the ego. I'm expecting Anthony to be quite an exhibition, something as if Canute were doubling in brass, once for the wind, and once for the sea. Anthony is so accustomed to regulating things that he takes any undesirable change in the weather as a personal insult. There's an awful lot of elasticity in sanity, my dear Valcour."

Valcour said absently: "Yes, isn't there?" He was staring at young John Bettle, who had just come in through the saloon door. John was sick-looking. There was a message blank in his hand.

"For you, Mr. Valcour," John said. He handed the blank to Valcour. He sat down at the table. "There's nothing coming through on the telephone at all. It was all I could do to catch the signals through the static. It took seven repeats." John looked very tired, very sick.

Valcour read the message. He was a very puzzled man. The body of the message said:

THE PAPERS IN HEDGLIN BRIEFCASE CONTAINED
REPORT ON PETER MOORE STOP ADVISE YOU QUES-
TION HIM CLOSELY CONCERNING HIS PAST STOP BEAR
IN MIND HE IS WAVERLY HEDGLINS HEIR END

The message was signed by the commissioner. Valcour folded it and put it in his pocket. "Something wrong, my dear Valcour?"

"It isn't wrong," Valcour said thoughtfully. "It's impossible."

CHAPTER TWENTY-EIGHT

AT A QUARTER AFTER TWO

...and at a quarter after some unspecified hour to-night I am going to be dead...

Carlotta sat on the edge of her bed and considered the thought dispassionately. Her cabin was in magnificent confusion. Everything movable had found its way to the floor and was in a state of constant motion with the eccentric rolling and pitching of the ship.

She thought: *If I bolt the door nothing can happen to me.* She needed sleep. Her eyes were thick with it and her skin was dry and hot from tiredness. *If I bolt the door* (she thought) *and put something against it I can lie down and get some sleep.* She stared at a make-up case sliding among other things past her feet. It wouldn't do any good to put anything against the door.

She looked at a diamond-and-platinum watch on her wrist. She held her wrist up so that she could look at the watch closely. She wished she had a bigger watch with larger hands so that she could see them without staring so closely.

Fourteen minutes after one o'clock. For two full minutes she did not move her eyes from the little hands of the watch. Not until they had passed the quarter-hour.

She thought: *There will be four more such quarter-hours to pass before the night is over.* Her eyes were quite thick and she rubbed them vigorously with hot dry fingers. The bolt was good. The bolt would stop anybody from coming in and getting at her while she took a little sleep. Not much, just a little sleep. A few minutes would set her up again—of sleep...

The knife was cold in her hot dry hand. She dropped it back again on the satin spread. She stared stupidly at the pillows. Just five minutes' sleep with her tired head cradled on those pillows. Bolts were not an unsolvable problem to anyone who was clever. And the person whom she expected—She sat suddenly much straighter, quite wakeful, and her eyes weren't thick any more. They were little-looking and calculatingly hard.

She made her way awkwardly across the cabin to a basin. Suitcases cluttered her feet, brushed her ankles, slithered past. She splashed cold water on her chalk-white face. She felt nervously energetic, refreshed. She gathered all the towels together, opened the door of the cabin's locker, and took out an armful of clothes; then she went back to the bed.

She turned back the covers and with the clothes and towels molded the shape of a body. She punched the pillows, pulled the covers up again, pressed them, arranged them. It was, she knew, heaven knows how old a trick. But it was real-looking. Very real. She made her way about and clicked out lights. She drew back the curtains of the ports. The cabin was black. She waited, holding onto the head of the bed, until her eyes accustomed themselves. Light filtered faintly through the ports from an awning lamp outside them on the deck. It was very real, the dummy. Like a person sleeping. Like a body deeply sleeping.

She thought: *I must light the lights again, and go out into the passage. I must walk along the passage. I must go to the bathroom. I must stay there for a while and then come back again. I must make some noise along the passage.*

She drew the curtains again across the ports and groped her way stumbling toward a dresser. Her hands found a lamp and clicked its switch. Pink filtered palely through its shade. She opened the cabin door and went out into the passage. It was easy to stumble and make noise on her way along the passage. Her hand consciously found and pressed sharply against one door as she passed it.

She went on to the bathroom, went inside, closed its door. White and cold and hard, the light was, in the bathroom. Like her cheeks and her excited, calculating, hard cold eyes. She forced herself to stay five minutes, then went back into the dim and empty passage again, and her hand in passing lurched against the same shut door.

Pale pinkness was incongruous with the disordered mess of her things and the cabin's furnishings. She closed and did not bolt its door. She stood for a moment with her back pressed against its panels, staring with her hard cold eyes, listening to heavy seas smashing in massed attack on plates outside the curtained ports.

She went over to the locker and assured herself that it was empty. She got on her knees and stared beneath the bed. She took a look at her watch. Twenty minutes to two. She thought: *Thirty-five minutes more to wait, to pretend to go back to sleep in.*

She clicked the light out on the dresser and drew back the curtains of the ports. Light filtered slowly in and objects developed form reluctantly. She stood for quite a while staring down on the bed. *It's a good dummy*, she thought. She went to the foot of the bed and sat down on the floor, close against the wall, leaning back against the bed, and her eyes fastened themselves carefully on the passage door, on the slender pencil of light at its base.

She thought: *That light will go out before the door starts to open. I'll know when the door is going to open because the light in the passage will first be put out. If I watch the strip of light I'll have plenty of warning.*

Her hot dry fingers closed gently on the knife. It was cold, the knife, and she let it stay on the floor beside her, jabbing its sharp point into the woodwork, leaving its handle convenient for her hot dry fingers.

Darkness intensified each smashing wave and shuddering of the straining ship sucking harshly at swift sinking crests before the helpless plunging wallow into distracted troughs. She thought: *The officers will be on watch on the bridge; everyone who is awake and on duty among the crew will be at their stations or on the bridge. The passage will be clear.*

She could not, in the darkness, see the passing minutes. Her thoughts were a millrace intervaled with blankness. It was hypnotic, the slender pencil of yellow light at the base of the passage door. Noises in their constant confusion grew monotonous, were a habit, were dulled from usage and ignored.

She thought: *It is easy to imagine things when it is dark; if I did not know I was alone in the cabin I would think that that little creaking came from the springs of the bed.*

That, she knew, was stupid. Realistic as the dummy was, it would not creak about in bed. Her eyes kept fixed on the pencil of light, so steady, so hypnotic, at the base of the passage door. They were ignorant of the bedclothes being gently lifted on the bed, of the dummy quietly, gently, lifting feet over the edge of the bed, of the dummy's knees in careful creeps inching along the cluttered noisy floor.

It was time, she thought, that the hands of her watch were nearing the quarter-hour. She reached her own hot hand out toward the knife. It closed on flesh.

PART FOUR

CHAPTER TWENTY-NINE

WIND

Valcour could not sleep. He lay dressed on top of the covers and felt that each staggering roll of the yacht would throw him from the bed. He located one shoe jammed beneath the wash basin, the other one was under a suitcase of Hedglin's, lopsided in a corner. He put them on and went on deck. Wind flattened him against the house and he made his way with greatest difficulty up to the bridge. He found Captain Jorgensen, legs apart and braced, at the starboard end of it.

"Quite a night, Captain." Wind whipped the words from his mouth. "As one seaman to another who isn't, what's the big idea?"

Captain Jorgensen did his best to grin reassuringly. He shouted: "You are right, Valcour. It is a good little blow." It was painful even to himself, that grin. He knew that about thirty minutes ago the mercury had been dangerously low. He had watched it swing far up the long tube, poise for a second, and then fall. Pumping. It was a hard thing to grin when the mercury in the glass was pumping.

Mr. Jones joined them, coming out of the darkness, and coming, for Mr. Jones, quite rapidly. He looked at Valcour and said: "Oh."

"Well, Mr. Jones?" Captain Jorgensen's voice had a worried edge.

"Twenty-eight point eighteen, Captain. Pumping. Sou'sou'east, full speed ahead."

"Changing our course?" Valcour said.

"We are trying to get as far away as we can from land, Valcour." Captain Jorgensen added: "Before it strikes."

"The hurricane?"

"What makes you say that, man?"

"Mr. Luke is under the impression that we are due for a hurricane."

Captain Jorgensen snorted loudly. "That man! I think he is the devil."

"We are, aren't we?"

Mr. Jones said laconically: "As you're liable to find it out for your-self in about ten minutes, Mr. Valcour, we are. You may have noticed that it's quite still."

"The lull before the storm?"

"Yes, Mr. Valcour. The very well known lull before the storm."

"I've been curious about hurricanes," Valcour said. "Don't you have to make all sorts of preparations?"

Captain Jorgensen was very steady and reassuring. "They are made."

Mr. Doorn added himself to their little group, tall and dour, his face a gray splotch in darkness. "Everyone is posted, Captain," he said.

"That is good, Mr. Doorn." Captain Jorgensen was fretful, staring with wide and sure and speculative eyes over the dodger. He said: "This stillness."

"What's liable to happen?" Valcour asked.

Mr. Doom's voice in the silence, the dead blackness, was singularly unpleasant. "The ordinary fate of a ship in a hurricane," he said, "is to have her plating opened or her hatches stove in or both. In God's good time she fills."

"Steady, gentlemen! Valcour, I will ask you to go at once to the saloon. I have already told the steward and the stewardess to waken the others and have them gather there. When convenient, I shall send one of my officers down to reassure them." His voice was sharp: "You will go quick, man!"

With a droning scream it struck them.

Sickeningly the *Crusader* lurched, as a body shot, heeled further, further, further still, like a beaten thing. Lay sodden. Ribbons of canvas weather stripping slashed Valcour's face while wetness smothered it, hard and thick and smashing on the yellow droning wind that the wetness which was not, he knew as it stung salt brine in spindrift between his lips, any rain.

Flattened smooth, the sea was, under that first slashing onslaught of screaming, drumming wind, shocked to sliced flatness, and Valcour inched his way, clinging wherever and to whatever he could cling, down the tilted bridge to its shelter side. He heard, as he passed them, Captain Jorgensen's great voice shout to Mr. Jones, as if it were a whisper: "She does not right herself—cargo in the hold has shifted—you will attempt to bring her through the wind. You will be quick, please, man. It's weight may straighten her out…"

You could breathe on the shelter side of the charthouse, a little, and Valcour made his way inside of it, into the cluttered confusion of its floor. The helmsman was knocked unconscious against a wall, torn from the wheel by that first vicious lurch, and Mr. Jones was plunging past him, climbing up the steeply tilted floor towards the wheel, saying loudly: "You can lend a hand here, Valcour."

The sea was again rising, swiftly, treacherously, increasing sickeningly the dangerous angle of the listed ship. They clung to the wheel together, Valcour and Mr. Jones, and heavily, with soggy lifelessness, the *Crusader* wallowed, nuzzled, swung with grunts and pain, by snoring inches up into the wind. "Steady now!" Mr. Jones shouted...

It was beautifully done. Through the screaming and the drumming she went, a few nervous successive shocks above her pounding, then tortuously back into the wind again, snoring head on up mountains with her list appreciably lessened, up and up and up on mountains that piled smashing on her forecastle with a run that went aft as whole water, heavy and solid, and destructive as a strong and stupid child, smashing everything smashable in its path, so powerful and heavy was this run.

"Better be satisfied with this," Mr. Jones said. "I'll hold her while you slap the helmsman back to his senses."

"Got her all right?"

"All right, Mr. Valcour."

Valcour found the helmsman already on his knees, swaying in dull bewilderment on his knees, attempting to stand.

"Are you all right?" Valcour helped him up.

The youngster grinned faintly. He said: "Oh, sure."

Valcour steadied him as they went back to the wheel.

"Can you handle it?" Mr. Jones asked.

"Yes, sir."

"Then hold her into the wind until I get back."

"Yes, sir."

Mr. Jones turned to Valcour. "I don't understand it," he said. "This limping. You'd think we were disabled. I'm going out to see if anything has happened to the Old Man. We should be driving full speed ahead. We should alter our course to get away from the storm center. You have to do that with these lousy circular storms."

Valcour battled his way after Mr. Jones, flattened like paper against the house, to where Captain Jorgensen was clinging at the center of the bridge.

"Any orders, sir?" Mr. Jones shouted. "What course?"

Captain Jorgensen shouted back: "You will keep her just as she is. For as long as you can you will keep her, please, straight into the wind." His shouts were whispers in that screaming drumming wind. "She does not answer her telegraph. I think there is a little trouble with her turbines. I think that maybe she will need some little repairs..."

CHAPTER THIRTY

STIFF AND RED AND PITCHING

White, shocked faces stared at wreckage in the saloon. "What a piano!" Freda said. And Helen Bettle's voice stated placidly: "It had just been tuned. The salt air is so bad for the strings, Mr. Valcour." While Wharton said: "My God!" and braced himself more firmly on the floor.

They were seated, all of them, on the floor, braced against anything solid that resisted the violent, eccentric motion of the yacht, and things swept clattering past them.

All but Carlotta.

Bettle said: "Where's Carlotta? Steward, where is Miss Balfé?"

Burke was clinging to a handful of wires from the piano. "I pounded on her door, Mr. Bettle, and yelled."

"Did she answer?" Bettle's voice was sharp.

"Couldn't say, sir. We lurched just then and it knocked me flat. I was out for several minutes, Mr. Bettle. Then I started pounding on the other doors, but everybody was up."

Freda said: "Up? I acted like a piece of popcorn just as it pops—" She caught one of Peter's feet as she started to slide, with the piano bench, across the floor. "Such a splendid anchor!" The opposite roll sent the top of her head violently into Peter's chest. "Where does the man get his strange powers of attraction?"

"My, uh, throat—"

She took her fingers from their clutch on the inside of Peter's collar and secured an arm. "Now we're nicely settled," she said.

John Bettle started to laugh. It was a funny laugh and contrasted oddly with his white face shocked with fright. He was across the room from Freda and Peter, staring at her as she leaned, so solid, so comfortable, so secure, in Peter's arm. John stopped laughing. He said: "Bless you, my children." His father's voice cut sharply, saying: "Stop it, John! We must find out at once why Carlotta hasn't joined us."

Bettle got to his feet, heavily, awkwardly, and Valcour and Burke joined him, followed him out of the wrecked saloon and aft along the crazily lunging passage. Bettle said ponderously: "She has been injured; thrown from bed and injured. This storm will not last long." He added with a strong and complacent finality: "There is nothing to worry about."

The door to Carlotta's cabin was jammed by a dresser that had rolled and blocked it. It took the combined strength of the three of them to force it open. It was pitch black inside the cabin and Burke groped for switches and lighted lights.

They saw her instantly, huddled on the floor at the foot of the bed. There was a strange rigidity about her; very rigid, very noticeable against the motion of almost everything else in the cabin. Valcour braced himself and lifted her. Blood was thick at her back. "Someone has knifed her," he said, "in the back. She is dead."

Bettle was unnerved. There were shocking loosenesses about his granite face, a flaccid helplessness of lips. Burke's somber eyes were tightened and steady with shocked hardness.

"I said," Burke said, "that there was murder in this ship."

They braced themselves against the sickening plunging, staring at dead Carlotta with her wet red back, and Mr. Jones came through the doorway from the passage with a correct smile badly frozen on his lips. It stayed there, that smile, while he stared with fright-wide eyes at Carlotta. "She's bleeding," he said.

Bettle said absently: "She is dead." He did not seem natural, Bettle, not like a conscious man at all. He was all over loose confusion, slack with uncertainties, and his voice had the querulous note of a complaining child. "Mr. Jones, please give my compliments to Captain Jorgensen and ask him at once to head for the nearest coastal port." The words dribbled faintly. He said:

"Savannah—Jacksonville—arrangements for a funeral—proper church—" and stopped, unwound.

Mr. Jones said awkwardly: "Sorry, Mr. Bettle. There's a little trouble with the turbines. They're doing their best to get them in shape. We've just enough power to keep her stem into the wind. And in any case, until this blow stops, we'd have to run for the open sea."

"Ah, yes." Bettle's sigh was slender. "This wind. The flowers, I think, had better come by plane..."

Bettle stared vacantly at Carlotta, bowed politely to the steward, and went out into the passage. They heard him lumbering and fumbling his way toward the door of his quarters, and Valcour said: "Better go with him, Mr. Burke."

"Yes, Mr. Valcour." It was almost a physical wrench, this tearing of his eyes from that wet red puddle. Burke muttered: "Knocked him clean on his beam ends, it did." They heard him add, just as he stumbled into the passage: "My God—bowed to me…"

Valcour looked sharply at young Jones. "Take it easy, Mr. Jones," he said. "Stop smiling that way."

"Smiling?" The idea was startling. "Never knew I was."

"I know you didn't."

"Shall I help you?"

"Help me?"

"Help you lift her onto the bed, Mr. Valcour."

"Not just yet."

Mr. Jones was deeply shocked. "You're not going to let her lie there on the floor?"

"Just for a minute. It is unfortunate that we have to harden ourselves to most of the decencies, in our business, Mr. Jones."

"I see." (He didn't. He didn't see anything at all, except that stiff thing with its sopping redness; so still and stiff and red in the middle of brutal pitching.)

"There are certain things that must be done in murder. I'll be as quick as I can." Valcour was at the bed, thoughtfully observing the state of its covers, looking at the odds and ends of clothing streeling from beneath them. At the towels. He said: "She made a dummy."

Mr. Jones was blank. "A dummy?"

"Yes. Then somebody took the place of the dummy. In bed." He carefully lifted the covers back entirely, and studied depressions. "Somebody without shoes, with clean dry slippers, or stockings, or socks, or with bare dry feet. All right, Mr. Jones, we can place her on the bed."

"Are you sure she's dead?"

"Yes. She knew that death was coming. Her shock of fright was terrific."

"She doesn't look frightened."

"The condition of the blood shows that death was recent, and yet rigor mortis has set in completely. Therefore she died under great shock." They placed Carlotta on the bed and covered her with a sheet.

"Shall I lash her down, Mr. Valcour?"

"It would be best."

Mr. Jones started ripping another sheet lengthwise, and Valcour searched the cabin for a knife. There was no knife, but a silk dressing gown was smeared where one had been wiped. Mr. Jones was shortly finished with lashings. He felt completely sick. He said: "Her watch stopped, Mr. Valcour, at a quarter past two."

…at a quarter after some unspecified hour…

Valcour went over to the bed. He felt frankly shaken. He examined the watch carefully, and felt much better. "Someone set this watch at a quarter after two. Whoever did it forgot to push the stem back in again." His smile was queer. "So much for ghosts," he said.

CHAPTER THIRTY-ONE

STREELING STRINGS TWIRL FILTHILY

Mr. Jones sucked a pencil and stared thoughtfully at the Log Book which he had rescued from the floor. The Log Book was wet and pretty badly torn. The windows of the chartroom were smashed in and a lashing rain added its confusion to the welter on the floor. The wind was coming through in a screaming fury. Hatch covers (Mr. Jones knew) had been torn off and flung into the sea, ventilators smashed, and winches wrecked. Water was pouring into the hold. He sucked his pencil, braced cramped legs more firmly, and thought of Carlotta: *She's a lucky woman to be out of this*. He added: *So soon*.

He wrote carefully, slowly, in the sodden Log Book:

> "At 4:32 A.M. Saturday, wind velocity 150 miles per hour, barometer 27.75, pumping violently, throwing indicator down to 27.60. Carlotta Balfé dead from knife wound in back. Body lashed to bed in her cabin. Assailant unknown. Ship unmanageable and heading southeast by east. Pounding heavily in rough seas. Damage caused to interior by driving rain. Crew bailing water out of saloons. Hatch covers gone and pumps working on water in hold. Turbines still undergoing repairs. Captain has estimated from precarious observations that storm vortex will pass directly over yacht if turbines are not fixed in time to make a run for it."

He closed the Log Book and jammed it into the pigeonhole of a rack. He put the pencil carefully back in his pocket. He muttered to the helmsman: "My God, what a life!" and started for the deck, where he found Captain Jorgensen, Burke, and Valcour pinned by the screaming wind against the house at the bridge's center.

Burke, too, was screaming; screaming into Valcour's ear: "Fire axe…positively vanished from its case…wanted it to chop loose a busted door…nothing could have wrenched it from its case…first it's my electric iron and now a fire axe…bunch of blooming crooks…"

Mr. Jones felt a little giddy. "We should worry," he shouted, "about a fire axe."

But Valcour did worry. He worried tremendously, trying to fit this new oddity into the general puzzle. He shouted at Burke: "Where was it hanging—the axe?"

"In the pantry of the officers' mess, up here on the boat deck."

Valcour's heart was suddenly cold. The boat deck. The deck on which were kept the lifeboats. He turned to Captain Jorgensen, got close to him, pressed his lips almost against his ear, and shouted: "Is there any chance that we may have to take to the boats?"

"Now? Dear man, even if we had to we could not launch them now."

"Later?"

"I have a feeling, Valcour, here,"—he thumped his chest—"that we shall come through this storm. We shall come through to good weather and smoother seas. It will be time enough then to think about the boats."

Valcour was persistent. "But if we do come through this, will we need to take to them?"

"I cannot tell. The water in the hold I can control if it is coming simply from the overbreaking seas, but if her plating is sprung, Valcour, I do not know."

Thin and feeble their gigantic shouts were in the screaming drumming wind.

"Captain, I am worried about the boats. Can they be examined without too much danger?"

"Now?"

"Now."

Captain Jorgensen's face streamed water. He stared with difficulty, intently, at Valcour, through streaming water. He shouted: "Mr. Jones, you will please inspect the boats."

Mr. Jones staggered inching along the bridge, gripped his way around the corner of the house, and suddenly, shockingly, the wind was still.

Quite still.

It was almost an impossibility to breathe. It was like breathing in a vacuum, a vacuum caused by strong suctions of the straight up-swinging wind.

Captain Jorgensen's voice was steady and strong. He said: "We are in the vortex of the storm."

Faint dawn-light rimmed the close-in circle of the sea, while smothering down on them was a lead-black lid, filthy and solid, with streeling fingers at its distant edges; dirty fingers streeling lazily, unwholesome little strings of twirling filth. Water spouts were sudden everywhere and the sea about them was pyramidal, reaching in that deadly unbreathable silence to stupendous heights that were crestless because there was no wind, catching the yacht up bodily and letting her down with savage crashes while water deluged incessantly.

Burke was a pallid sheet, and Valcour said: "How long does this last, Captain?" (That weird, clear voice could not be his in this strange stillness!)

Tears were frankly streaming down Captain Jorgensen's miserable face. "The poor little thing," he shouted, good and loud. "I can do nothing for her. Until her turbines are fixed I can do nothing for her. Not one damn thing. Last?" He turned confusedly to Valcour. "I cannot tell that, man. Perhaps for half an hour."

Mr. Jones was with them. Mr. Jones was shaken. He said to Captain Jorgensen: "Three boats have been torn loose from their davits, sir. The fourth has been stove in with an axe."

CHAPTER THIRTY-TWO

BIRDS CLING IN STILLNESS

The yacht was a curious aviary in this profound and sinister stillness. All manner of sea birds clung to her in exhaustion from their battle with the storm, snatching this moment of rest before the storm vortex should have passed and, drumming screaming madness, crash out at them again. Valcour fumbled his way against the violent lurching, down to the main deck, and into the saloon.

The saloon was thick with it, this dreadful stillness, and Anthony Bettle's voice, from where he stood clinging to the smashed piano, was droning, droning, droning:—"*...and so we thank Thee, our Father, and beg Thee in Thy infinite goodness and mercy to—*"

"*Stop it! Stop it!*" screamed John. Choking, John's voice was, very thick, very upset.

"*—to grant that we may outlive this storm and find safe harborage, the better to pursue Thy works and...*"

Wharton explained to his sister: "The wind has Stopped, my dear Helen, because of the circular motion of the hurricane. It hasn't stopped, really, at all. It's going up. We are now passing through the storm's center."

Helen said placidly: "I'm frightened, Wharton. My head hurts. If it has stopped, why do you say it hasn't? Why do you say it's going up?" She turned to Barlowe, who was sick and white on the floor beside her. "Don't you find that confusing, Mr. Barlowe?" ("*...we who are Thy children here on earth, that the fruit of Thy great teachings may not vanish from its surface and he...*") "I do wish that Anthony would stop occasionally. Don't you think there ought to be some punctuation in prayers? I know that during our services at Saint Christopher's Mr. Osterholter always interpolates a musical effect whenever he..."

"Listen, Freda," Peter was saying. "How about shifting over to the other arm? This one is dead."   And Miss Singlestar was a fear-stricken rabbit saying over and over again in her empty, rattling, little head: *In the midst of life we are in death in the midst of life we are in death in the midst of life we are in death*, over and over and over again, while her teeth were painful from jerking showers of sharp little clicks.

"Papa," Freda called.

Horatio Barlowe stared at his daughter biliously. He said, with great difficulty: "What?"

"Peter called me Freda."

"Well, I could tell him a few good things to call you besides Freda." Barlowe collapsed back again onto the floor.

Fluidly, ceaselessly, droning from the smashed piano: "*...and so, dear Lord, if it should meet with Thy purpose that we come by drowning into Thine arms, then let us...*"

The ragged pulse of the turbines' beat grew suddenly very even and strong, the floor seemed noticeably to leap beneath them as the yacht, with increasing momentum, plunged full speed ahead. They were all bewildered, very frightened, at first not grasping the significance of the lunge, the swirl, the change of course, this plummet-dart plunging obliquely from the path of the storm.

There was an unearthly blaze on Anthony Bettle's face. He lowered himself stiffly onto his knees. "*Our Lord*," he said, "*we thank Thee.*" He dropped still further onto the floor. Lay flat. He slept.

Barlowe raised his head and said: "Once more we seem to be off." His deep and soft and hearty laugh ended in a sick groan, and his head struck loosely back upon the floor.

Helen stared down at Barlowe tranquilly. She said: "I wonder whether some aspirin would help. I never could understand these cults. About people who make a religion out of sitting on floors. I think it's most uncomfortable. Or would you suggest some spirits of ammonia, Wharton?"

Wharton looked at his sister admiringly. "Your mind, my dear Helen, offers about the only lucid physical explanation known to man of the true mechanics of a Mexican Jumping Bean. As for Barlowe, I suggest a shroud, taken three times a day immediately after his meals."

Barlowe said weakly: "With underdone lilies," and young Jones came bursting in, beaming, saying: "Cheer up, folks, the old tub's off again like a bat out of hell." He caught something tranquilly fishy in Helen Bettle's eye and added formally: "I mean to say, that is, we're again under full power, we're making a cut to get out of the path of the storm, and the captain advises you to guard against accidents from the motion that will be briefly ahead of us until we clear the edge."

Mr. Jones turned around and was out on deck, and the wind ripped the door from his hand with a crash, as the screaming drumming madness leaped with a smash of gunfire on the yacht's flank.

They clung to each other a little tighter, Peter and Freda, and he said to her: "Just a little longer now." She could feel the warmness of his lips, his breath against her ear, the warmness of his arm about her; very loose and warm and complete her body felt with his arm about her, and she was unconscious of the drumming scream, the plunging, the sick, sick heave and plunging, the thoroughbred forward-surging lunges of the shaken ship, just warmness and stillness and deafness and blindness, and a deeper settling close in that securing arm.

There was no more talking, so great was the futility of having anything to say. Anthony Bettle's hand, in sleep, hooked itself firmly about a leg of the smashed piano, and Helen thought of box springs, of eiderdown, of her own immense headache, and of John. John looked, she thought, like a terrified child. Not for years had she noticed so much helpless youngness about him. She hoped that he wasn't going to be too hurt about Freda. It was so obvious about Freda. Peter and Freda. Helen was distinctly relieved and glad of it. Even if Freda's mother hadn't been a pickpocket, such stories had a habit of getting around and of never being entirely disproven. She wondered whether Miss Ketcham's could counteract a pickpocket. Miss Ketcham's could counteract a lot of things. But pocket-picking...

Wharton leaned close to Valcour. He made his voice loud enough to be heard and no louder. "What have they done with her?" he said.

"Lashed her to the bed."

A heavy table tottered, poised sickeningly, crashed on its side.

Wharton's eyes were no longer cynical. "It's a wretched picture," he said. "When you think..."

CHAPTER THIRTY-THREE

WAXWORKS OF LIVING DEAD

Cold, the new wind was, with ice on its crest; screaming, yelling incessantly, with the hurricane drone as a deep and dreadful base, and the yacht was a waxworks of sick and inarticulate people, so bloodless that they were like living dead.

At eight o'clock in the morning Mr. Jones again sucked his pencil and wrote in the pulpish Log Book:

"Glass 29.40, pumping, wind easing a little."

At nine-thirty:

"Glass 29.50, wind moderating to 60 miles per hour, storm breaking up, wind and weather improving rapidly. The ship is leaking badly. Impossible as yet to determine source. Pumps going to capacity. Heading full speed south-southwest."

At a quarter after ten sun flashed through broken scud and the motion had lessened to a point where walking was no longer a gymnastic art.

Bettle's quarters had been put back into some degree of order. They were bare-looking, very stripped—so many of their furnishings had been irreparably smashed and had been thrown over the side—they were as a person is who has been seriously ill from an enduring shock. As was Bettle. He looked like his quarters, as if a good deal of his strength and masterful dominance had been jettisoned, with the ruined fittings, over the side.

Valcour said to him: "She was of such importance to you?"

"Importance? Carlotta?" There was no longer any private racing to Bettle's thoughts: rather was there an annoying and confused groping through a murky blankness. He spoke hesitantly, not weighing words, but searching after them as after unfamiliar and unfindable things. "I shall try to tell you, Mr. Valcour, what Carlotta meant to me."

Valcour thought: *It's himself he is trying to tell. He is a boxer coming out of a pretty final knockout blow, and is trying to establish himself with life again.* Valcour said: "You found her an essential part of your project?"

"Yes. An essential part. Every man needs some element of personal contact with his source of supply, if he is to succeed in any business."

"Yes, Mr. Bettle?" (*This groping and childlike fingering of forgotten things...*)

"My business, Mr. Valcour, is with God." Valcour stared steadily at Bettle, thinking: *This must be madness.* But it wasn't madness, not a bit. He thought: *There is no more madness in a man dealing with God than there is in a man dealing with beauty or with any abstraction.* Men capture beauty and translate it into tangible and visual *form* in innumerable ways: on canvas, with sheaths of stone, with melody, with light. And such things, from their intimate familiarity, were not looked upon as madness. So should it be, too, with Godliness. *Kind men*, he thought, *are men who deal directly with God.* In Bettle's case it was simply a dealing which wealth and power had elevated to a somewhat fantastic and abnormal degree. Valcour said: "Miss Balfé afforded you that contact?"

"Why not?"

Valcour shrugged slightly. "Spiritualism has always held a stronger touch of the earth, for me, than of heaven."

"But it's a gateway. Don't you see, Mr. Valcour? It is a gate."

"To God?"

"Certainly, to God. It brings us into communication with those who must, in their spiritual state, be in direct touch with God."

It was not a lesson learned by rote: rather was it a genuine and sincere belief. It was at least a more intelligent one, Valcour thought, than the common belief in an occult efficacy of knocking wood. He said: "Who hates you on this yacht?"

"Hates me?"

"Hates you enough to have killed Carlotta."

"No one who is here with me hates me, Mr. Valcour." Bettle was still the child in a much too big body. "I would know if anyone hated me. One does. There is a physical something about hate, when it's near you, that you can feel. I've run into a good deal of hate in my lifetime. But it isn't here." Bettle was sunk again in the deep and miserable morass of Carlotta's death. He said: "I miss her very much."

Valcour said quietly: "The storm will have damaged the copper stills."

"Undoubtedly."

"Then the cargo was copper stills?"

"Certainly." (*How replaceable such inanimate things were; how wretchedly unreplaceable was Carlotta, was the illusive motive power of any flesh and bone and blood!*) "Copper stills."

"Why, Mr. Bettle? Why copper stills? If you'll forgive me for being blunt, what possible connection is there between serving God and copper stills?"

"You are no doubt aware of the tactical value of fighting the devil with evil, more modernly, of fighting fire with fire." Bettle's mind was clearing, regaining a grip on its normal shrewdness. "In your profession, Mr. Valcour, you are accustomed to condone the minor offenses of certain criminals in order to employ such criminals as informers against their fellows, and yet you are fighting all facets of crime."

"I see. I see your premise as a generality. But the details, Mr. Bettle?"

Bettle was rapidly becoming himself again; there was almost a visible inflation, a definite strengthening of manner and of voice. "I see no necessity for going into them, Mr. Valcour."

"Then you are blind; either ignorantly or willfully blind. There have been two murders done on this yacht. I have no official standing here but I do have the common right of every man, and *that is the right of self-preservation.*"

"Self-preservation?"

"Mr. Bettle, unless I can get to the bottom of this affair before tonight there will be twenty-six more attempted murders on this yacht."

Bettle was bewildered with calculations. "That would leave just one person," he said.

"The murderer would escape."

"Mr. Valcour, this is insanity."

Valcour thought for a moment. He said: "Will you do something for me, Mr. Bettle?"

"What?"

"If I give you my reasons for what you quite naturally have accepted as an insane statement, and if you find them at all convincing, will you back me up? Will you talk?"

Bettle's look was very searching. "I am neither a fool nor a stupid man, Mr. Valcour," he said. "I'll talk."

CHAPTER THIRTY-FOUR

THE WIG

Captain Jorgensen, too tired to be tired, was standing squarely on the starboard end of the bridge. The last resources of his great reserve strength were all that kept him there, staring down through the sun's hot noonday blaze at his stripped ship, so bare, as places are after locusts in destructive swarms have visited them; white and bare like bones of trees that have been eaten even of their bark; white thin nakedness in a petulantly deep and calm blue sea. Sinking.

Not from any great gash was the *Crusader* so gently, so very imperceptibly sinking right from underneath his squarely planted feet (as she might have from collision or the wrenching shock of a derelict or reef) but from a thousand little places. He thought: *All over she is leaking, every plate in her dear and weary little body is sprung, and hour after hour she will drink in tricklets until she has drunk her fill. I think she is as tired as I am. Then we will sink.*

He said to Valcour: "You are a man, dear Valcour, whose life has been lived with danger. You have learned to keep hold of your head. I will tell you a thing of which even my own officers are not yet fully aware. We are sinking. Every plate in our hull has been sprung by punches of the wind and seas. We are taking water faster than the pumps can pump it out. I have made calculations and am heading directly for the major lanes of coastwise traffic. We could not, you see, have time to reach the shore."

How easily, Valcour thought, *seamen go in for weeping*. He said: "You are considering an SOS?"

Captain Jorgensen produced a fine big handkerchief and blew his nose vigorously. "Let me show you," he said, "our situation. I have insisted that young Meddletree get over his nonsense about injuries and lawsuits. He is in the wireless shack now."

"Sending an S O S?"

"Not yet. I am having him broadcast a general inquiry call to find out what ships are near by." Captain Jorgensen sighed heavily and added: "Should it be by chance that a ship is near by."

"We're as close to going under as that?"

"No, there is no immediate closeness. She will not fill for many hours. Maybe not for ten or twelve hours will she drink up her fill."

"But isn't that time enough, with any sort of a break?"

"That is just it. We are not now in usual conditions. Traffic in all of this area will be scattered heaven knows where. Storm warnings will have sent them running to shelter, far off their normal courses, out to the open sea. There is one chance in millions, dear Valcour, that a single vessel will be near enough to join us, and there is then an even chance that that single ship will be as crippled as ourselves."

Something in Valcour's mind clicked, nagging at him irritatingly. There was something (he thought) that was waiting to be remembered—urgently—desperately. He said: "What will we do?"

"If Sparks does not get a satisfactory response, I will see what can be done about constructing rafts. They will be pretty useless things, Valcour, but there is a little comfort even in a useless thing when a man is clinging onto life."

"Can't the last boat be repaired?"

"You have not noticed?"

"Noticed?"

"It is gone, swept over as we came out of the storm." Captain Jorgensen stared hard down at the deep blue waters. "Its lines did not tear loose. They were cut, man, with a knife." His fists were clenched painfully. He said: "Why should such a thing be done? It is not only murder for the rest of us, it is a seeking after suicide for the doer himself."

"Captain, suppose you had a choice between certain death in the electric chair, or a gamble for life with a disaster at sea, which would you choose?"

"No matter if death in each way was certain, I would choose the sea. But this deliberate murdering—"

"I do not think that the murder of Waverly Hedglin was deliberate. I think it was an impulsive reaction to some shock and not at all premeditated. I think certain features of it were simply grasped at because they were opportune. I *do* think that the murder of Carlotta Balfé was both deliberate and premeditated; follow-up murders usually are. And I believe, Captain, that the murders which are planned to occur during the foundering of this yacht will be selective murders, with number one man on the list being myself."

"Dear man!"

"Let's look at the probable picture. I am not familiar with a foundering, but I imagine there must necessarily be an amount of strong self-interest, or concentrative interest on the special job at hand—either the saving of one's own life, or the saving of another's. The sea becomes a common enemy, and all thoughts are directed wholly and naturally towards it. There are two possibilities: either a ship reaches us in time to stand by and transfer us in her boats, or we are compelled to take to the water and to keep afloat with lifebelts, or cling to such makeshift rafts as are prepared, until a ship can reach those who are left of us and pick us up. You will naturally keep in touch with any ship that answers your call, and give them your position right up to the end, will you not?"

"Surely, man."

"Then consider the picture from either angle: no matter how we do it, we abandon the ship and she sinks. There will unquestionably be confusion. Murder can be done, and is planned to be done, during that confusion, and the bodies and the evidence will vanish with the yacht. You have no idea of the amount of evidence required to convict a person circumstantially of murder."

Captain Jorgensen was staring harder than ever down at the deep blue water. His face was very drawn and gray. "There is one thing in your picture that the murderer did not think of," he said. "Yes?"

"Look."

Valcour, too, looked down into the deep blue water. Long and lazy and ugly, the thing was. "Shark, isn't it?" he said.

"Yes, my dear Valcour. It is a funny thing about such sharks. They seem to know." Captain Jorgensen's huge fists could get no tighter. "I think I could die better if first I could get at that man."

"I'll have him for you to-night, Captain."

"Dear man, you know who he is?"

"No, but things are clearer now than they were before."

"Why, Valcour?"

"Because I have just found out that Waverly Hedglin himself was bald, and wore a perfect wig."

PART FIVE

CHAPTER THIRTY-FIVE

WHITE, STRIPPED, AND BARE

Lunch was a little mélanged, but still a miracle on the part of the chef (his galley was a clutter of battered copper sloshed with salt water), and the dining saloon at least had stability.

"This soup," Wharton said, "should be dedicated to Mahatma Ghandi. The tax on it in India would put it in the class of green turtle."

Barlowe's laugh was deep and soft and hearty, and his lips were mechanically benevolent again. He said: "We could theme-song it with Down Where the Gumbo Meets the Sea."

Staring dreadfully, they were (Helen Bettle and Miss Singlestar and Peter), at Carlotta's empty chair, staring with shocked and furtive glances, and John and Freda followed their looks with sidewise glances toward it. Anthony Bettle, at the table's end, ignored it ponderously, and Valcour from his place at Helen's left could not see it at all.

Valcour thought: *One of these people killed Carlotta and isn't looking at an empty chair, but is looking at a woman's knifed body lashed by torn sheets to a bed.* He wondered how they would react if they knew, as he knew, that the yacht was sinking, if this reverse-swing of congratulatory light-headedness at their escape from the hurricane (for they were feeling it, in spite of the ugly shadow of Carlotta's deadness they were feeling it) were suddenly effaced by the knowledge that the yacht, so very gently from beneath them, was sinking. He remembered a fire where many people had lunged with heels across a woman's face in panic. He said: "In the future I'll always insist on a dash of the brackish."

Helen said tranquilly: "It isn't unpleasant and it's very new. Wharton says that everything is new. I suppose he says so just to be contrary, because the accepted belief seems to be that nothing is. He says that the oldest things are really the newest because they've undergone the greatest change. There really does seem to be some sense to that. I wish I could find it." She thought: *John is still sick.* As she looked at it down the length of the table, where he sat between Freda and Carlotta's empty chair, John's skin was unhealthy in color and drawn, as Anthony's was;

sick-looking skin, the way skin gets from some obscure and baffling disease. That young Peter Moore, on the other hand, with his ugly truculence on full-blooded cheeks, dark and fresh and red, and his odd hurt staring across the table at Freda as if he couldn't make her out and didn't want to, really, or else could make her out too well… "Yes, Mr. Barlowe, it is a little bit like being born again. If one could remember the first time."

Wharton "My-God"-ed her from Barlowe's other side and said: "Helen is the only person I know who consistently ignores the fact that white is composed of all the colors."

Helen said: "Is it?" She thought: *Both John and Anthony ought to take something. Perhaps in the medicine chest, if there were some of the tasteless kind...* She said to Valcour: "I don't like to know things like that; what happens underneath things. In my day they never studied physiology at school. It wasn't nice. I like surfaces. I like to think of white as being white. I think you ought to look at things the way they're meant to be looked at, or all the bother of making them look that way goes for nothing."

Wharton was awestruck and murmured: "Madame Plato!" He included the entire table. "My sister," he announced, "is performing in togas. Her next impersonation will be Nero on Humanism, or Why the Holy Roman Empire was Neither."

Burke said bleakly: "Chicken, sir?"

Wharton eyed the dish. "It's chicken sponge cake, steward."

"Yes, sir. Will you have some, Mr. Luke?"

"Good God, yes. I wouldn't miss the sensation for worlds. There is something about the consistency of this pullet that is positively unique."

Miss Singlestar managed a thin and unconvincing smile. How swiftly different, she thought, things could be; different from hopes, from plans, from nicenesses imagined! It was confusedly astonishing to her: the unpurchasableness of pleasantness, of quiet and pleasant living. Only the machinery for it could be bought; the motive power had to be supplied by simple things inside of one's self, and you either had them or not. This lovely yacht (what there was left of this lovely yacht) and nice undissipated people. Yet there was that empty chair.

Right across the table from her it was, that empty chair. And Mr. Bettle, on her right, was the miserable and unhappy owner of all this lovely background built so carefully, so beautifully, for pleasant niceness. It couldn't be just goodness (the requisite motive power). Mr. Bettle had lots of goodness. He should have shaved. The gray stubble on his gray cheeks and chin made him look years older. He had a tramp look, really. One of the country's richest men. He could use a new blade each day in his razor, if he cared to. A young cousin of hers had told her once that he (the cousin) managed to use the same blade for ten times running and had figured out for her how much that saved him in a year. Almost thirty dollars. The income on about six hundred dollars at a safe percent.

And young John Bettle, the heir to all this purchasing power of niceness, looked so miserable and unhappy, too. She wondered whether Freda would marry him. She stared at John's stark wretched haggardness and wondered whether she'd like Freda to marry him, whether Freda's livingness wouldn't be quite quickly sapped into his misery... She wondered what it was, what special misery was ravaging so nakedly his sick young face... This brilliant match... She said automatically to Burke: "Thank you, steward," and helped herself to a morsel of curious chicken.

Burke kept on his way around the table. There was a nasty empty feeling in the pit of his stomach. Same as when the *Empress of Ulu* had gone down in the south Atlantic. He disliked founderings. Some mess or other always came up about the boats. He remembered the *Empress's* Number Seven having dumped, among others, two children and their mother into the water because of a faulty davit. The nasty hollering still bothered him sometimes... The mother and the scared screaming children...blotted out wetly, in muffles. Well, this time they'd miss that, he thought, not unbitterly. There weren't any boats. Lot of silly rafts they were knocking together up on the forward deck. Rafts, besides being inherently inconvenient, had no room for duffel. He'd have to wear the suit on his back. He could take his pins—six scarf pins weighed nothing at all—and he'd change right after this lousy lunch into his blue serge. He reviewed biliously precisely what salt water did to blue serge. Never got it out. Never. "No chicken? No, sir?"

Freda took chicken. She could feel John at her left (chickenless) the way you feel certain vibrations. The air was sort of psychical about him. She thought insanely: *It's Carlotta coming through him at me from that empty chair.* She said to Peter: "Since when the diet?"

Peter stared at her briefly over an emptied plate and said nothing. Freda didn't speak to him again. Just sat quietly and ate strange chicken. She felt bruised about Peter. As if he'd punched her. There had been (she was sure of it) a sense of unity between them during the storm, that needing-oneness which she flatly knew was love. So few things really were required, she thought, to fall in love. Time meant nothing, in the sense of any lengthy knowing of a person. Or looks. Something just dissolved inside of you, very suddenly and unreasoningly. Something that would never quite solidify again. You minded some people touching you. Others, you wanted to. Like Peter's arm. She never could feel smart in Peter's arm. He had taken it away. Definitely and quite finally he had taken his arm away. She had thought at the time: *He has just remembered something*. She stopped eating chicken. She was sick of chicken. She said to Valcour: "I wouldn't give two cents, sir, for your thoughts."

Valcour smiled agreeably. "Then you're a poor bargain hunter," he said.

"They're deep? Very costly and very deep?"

"Unplumbable."

"That word sounds like one of Commander Byrd's Antarctic discoveries."

Barlowe said: "Or an Eskimo dish."

"My father, Mr. Valcour, has a single-track mind. He certainly inherited no versatility from me."

"You mean, dear," Helen said placidly, "that you inherited no versatility from him. Or is it the other way around? I mean yours comes from your mother." Helen was suddenly confused.

Wharton said: "Our little Helen is back with us again, folks. No more togas."

"Dessert, sir?"

Wharton stared with pleased suspicion at the dish Burke was offering. "What is it?"

"I couldn't rightly say, Mr. Luke."

"It's dealer's choice."

"With,"—Barlowe joined Wharton in his inspection—"bananas wild."

"There is a bit of banana about it, sir."

"There are lots of bits of banana," Wharton said.

"Yes, Mr. Luke."

"In fact it's all bits. I've rarely seen a bittier dessert. The chef ought to call it Havoc."

Barlowe said: "What holds it together?"

"I couldn't say, sir."

"What, no sauce to hold it together? Just picture it, please, in transit."

"I could inquire, Mr. Barlowe."

Wharton said: "Do." He helped himself to the bitted bananas. "There will be something subtly fascinating about the sauce that can hold this dessert together."

"Sauce by that maestro, that master couturier, LePage?"

"Exactly, my dear Barlowe. Sauce pasta-a-la-LePage."

While the yacht, thought Valcour, *is gently sinking from tricklets beneath our feet*. He said: "I wonder whether it would be agreeable for all of you to join me, say a quarter of an hour or so after luncheon, in the saloon?"

They were still.

Bettle said: "An inquiry?"

Valcour said almost casually in the muscle-aching stillness: "We must arrive at some conclusion in regard to Carlotta Balfé's death."

CHAPTER THIRTY-SIX

SO PATIENT IN THE DEEP BLUE WATERS

Valcour waited until the rest had left the dining saloon. He wanted to talk with Burke. He said: "Mr. Burke, between nine-thirty o'clock and midnight of the night we sailed did anyone give you instructions about not wishing to be disturbed?"

"Disturbed?""Yes, you know the sort of thing I mean: wanting to stay in their cabin—locking its door—headache—some business to attend to—wanting to take a rest."

Burke transferred his thoughts from salted blue serge and six scarf pins to that eternity-ago-seeming night the yacht had sailed. "Come to think of it, Mr. Valcour, there was."

"Thank you, Mr. Burke."

Valcour hurriedly left the dining saloon and Burke stared after him absently, thinking: *There are more nuts on this ship than you can shake a stick at—he never even asked the party's name.*—Now—blue serge—why not the gray checked one? The effect of salt water on gray wool… wool…good God, *no*, not wool…blue serge…serge…

Valcour made his way immediately up to the boat deck and into the wireless room. He felt electric, as he always felt when, like the tumblers of a lock, the seemingly disassociated aspects of a problem were falling smoothly into place. It had clicked. That thing, which had been wanting to be remembered, had quite suddenly clicked.

He found Captain Jorgensen standing at the operating desk beside young Meddletree. Meddletree was very white-lipped and tense. He was sending a message and the room was filled with the subtle, swift *shush-shush* of the set's quenched gap.

Captain Jorgensen came over to Valcour. His careful whisper was an approximation of a normal tone of voice. "Valcour," he said, "we are in luck. The *Eastern Coast*, a cargo vessel of the Blue Funnel Line, is altering her course to join us at the quickest converging point. If our mutual calculations are correct, we should meet in time for a safe and easy transfer." Captain Jorgensen was flushed with solid, with blessed, hope;

very secure and assured again. There was a bubblingness about him. He said: "I am full of bubbles. You cannot dream of the responsibility."

"I can appreciate it fully, Captain."

"These dear people—all of these dear people…" Tears were in order again, and Captain Jorgensen indulged in them whole-heartedly. "Rafts," he said, with happy wetness, "I am having some constructed from the doors and various things just in case there should be a little slip-up and we should be compelled to abandon ship and take to the water for a little while. You see, dear man, the *Crusader* should be able to stay afloat for about four hours more, and the *Eastern Coast* should join us within three hours and a half."

"You are going to keep in constant communication with her?"

"Yes. Every half hour for a while and then, toward the finish, each single minute. The channels of the air are cleared for us of interference. Everyone, dear Valcour, is working to help us even if they can only do so by their stillness. It is a beautiful thing, this deep and neighborly friendship of the sea. My blood is wine."

Valcour was thoughtful. "Would it be permissible," he asked, "to get in touch with the commissioner by phone, during one of the half-hour stretches?"

"You will forgive me, Valcour, for saying no. In an emergency of this nature, you will appreciate that every other consideration must go by the boards. To telephone would involve different wave-length channels entirely, and for too long a time it would cut us off from communication with the *Eastern Coast*. I could not, much as I would like to, dear man, risk it. If you wish, you may send a message by straight wireless. That, I think, could be with comfort sandwiched in."

"That is good of you, Captain. It is important. I shouldn't have bothered you otherwise."

"I know it. I know it." Captain Jorgensen was on rubber. He said: "What joy!"

Valcour took a message blank from the rack. He wrote, in the department's simplest code:

EROOM RETEP GNINR ECNOC THGIN TSALK COLCO
NEVES FOEGA SSEMR UOYTA EPERD NAKLA TOTRE
HPARG ONETS NILGD EHGNI CROFF OTLUS ERYLE
TAIDE MMIES IVDAX

He addressed the message to the commissioner and signed his name. He gave it to Meddletree and said: "I'd appreciate your letting me have the answer as soon as it arrives. It will come through in code. It is a very simple code and will not require any repeats. I mean, by that, that any slight errors of reception on your part will be of no consequence. I will be in the saloon."

"Yes, Mr. Valcour."

Valcour went with Captain Jorgensen out onto the deck. They stood for a moment by the rail, staring down at the deep blue waters suffused with hot bright sun.

"They're still with us, I see," Valcour said.

Long and lazy and ugly, they were, effortlessly convoying the settling ship, waiting so patiently in the deep blue waters.

Captain Jorgensen was not depressed. "Sharks no longer worry me, dear Valcour. I have that feeling—here, inside of me—that tells me we will make safe harbor. Our rafts, if we should have to use them, will be good and sound. You will forgive me if I leave you? I must arrange the things we have to transfer. We will take the Log Book and such instruments and duffel as there may be room for in the boats of the *Eastern Coast*. It may be that there will be time for two or several trips, in which case we can take everything." Captain Jorgensen looked briefly disturbed. "That carafe in the safe, if it should not in the pounding have been quite smashed, and that piece of wicker with the blood, they should go?"

"If possible, Captain."

"I will see to it that they go."

"Thank you. I would like your opinion on just one thing."

"Yes, Valcour?"

"When riding at anchor, could a person climb aboard here by way of the anchor chain?"

Captain Jorgensen stared at him oddly. "Yes, Valcour," he said, "I think a man could."

Valcour went down to the main deck. He stood for a moment beside one of the saloon ports, looking carefully in. Everyone was assembled. He went aft along the deck and into the passage of the after-house. He opened one of the cabin doors and went inside. He went at once to the cabin's locker and flashed his electric torch minutely about it. He took a penknife from his pocket and sliced a sliver from the locker's wall. He left the cabin and started forward to join the others in the saloon.

The message he had sent by wireless to the commissioner was decodable by the simple process of running all the letters together, from their arbitrary division into groups of five, by eliminating the final X, which simply brought the last group up to the requisite number of five letters, and then by reversing the entire result:

ADVISEIMMEDIATELYRESULTOFFORCING   HEDG-
LINSTENOGRAPHERTOTALKANDREPEAT   YOURMES-
SAGEOFSEVENOCLOCKLASTNIGHT CONCERNINGPE-
TERMOORE

or:

ADVISE IMMEDIATELY RESULT OF FORCING HEDG-
LIN STENOGRAPHER TO TALK AND REPEAT YOUR
MESSAGE OF SEVEN OCLOCK LAST NIGHT CONCERN-
ING PETER MOORE

Valcour thought, as his hand reached out for the knob of the saloon
door: *I wish that I knew the motive for these singularly pitiful crimes.*

CHAPTER THIRTY-SEVEN

A LIAR LIES

There was a distinct grouping effect of the people in the saloon. Rather two groups and (Valcour thought) one singleton. The Betties formed one, with Anthony as its center, having Helen Bettle and John pressing close on either side of him, of his bewildered and shaken strength, like props that were replacing a removed support. Wharton, too, was of this group, immaculate, tidily neat, and somewhat subdued, with a dash of the small-boy-at-church look about him.

Across the saloon from them was Freda, flanked by Barlowe and Miss Singlestar.

Peter was ugly in a corner. Pointedly isolated and alone.

Valcour said to him abruptly: "Mr. Moore, I received the following wireless message last night at seven o'clock from the commissioner. It states: *The papers in Hedglin briefcase contained report on Peter Moore. Advise yon question him closely concerning his past. Bear in mind he is Waverly Hedglin's heir.* That's the message, Mr. Moore. What about it?"

Somebody's breathing was noticeable in the absolute stillness and Valcour stared curiously at Bettle, listening to that emphatic and troubled breathing.

Helen said: "I don't think Mr. Moore has a past." Helen was feeling suddenly and irrationally sorry for Peter. She was deciding that she liked him. She didn't believe that that would be possible if Peter had a past. Helen was quite sure of her instincts. If you relied on instincts implicitly it took an awful lot of the bother out of living. She thought: *He looks so lonesome over there. I wish he would come over here and sit with us.*

Color was leaving Peter's face, like something fading quickly. He said: "I don't know what about it, Mr. Valcour."

"You are your uncle's heir?"

"He has told me so."

Valcour kept looking at Peter thoughtfully. "There is no happening or detail in your life that you feel should be disclosed, that might prove of assistance to this inquiry?"

"No."

"Did you kill your uncle?"

"No."

"Do you wish to see his killer brought to justice?"

"Yes."

"Then will you be good enough to tell me, Mr. Moore, whom it was you *did* see on the boat deck shortly before the wireless man was knocked into unconsciousness by a blow on the head."

The color was gone entirely from Peter's skin. He said: "I saw two people, Mr. Valcour."

"They were together?"

"Yes."

"Who were they, please?"

"I wasn't very close to them. I could hear them better than I could see them. The wind carried their voices pretty clearly."

"Who do you think they were, Mr. Moore?"

"I thought that one of them was John Bettle, and the other one was Miss Barlowe." Peter kept his eyes deliberately from looking at Freda. "What did you hear them saying?"

"It was a proposal. A proposal of marriage. It was refused."

"Miss Barlowe refused to marry him?"

"No, Mr. Valcour. It was he who refused to marry Miss Barlowe."

Freda said in the beastly stillness: "That is a lie."

Barlowe was apoplectic and shouted: "I'll thrash you for that, you young puppy!"

Peter said: "Go ahead. I hope it is a lie."

"Gentlemen, there is nothing to be gained by forcing a scene." Valcour's voice was quieting. He looked at John. "What have you got to say about it?"

John's face was as pale as Peter's. "I think you know how I feel, Mr. Valcour, about Freda. It isn't only a lie. It's stupid. If Freda will marry me, I'll be the happiest man on earth."

Freda looked stonily at Peter. She said slowly: "Thank you, John. I will." And promptly burst into tears.

Freda cried very seldom, but when she did she was very businesslike and made a good job of it, generally ending the performance up in a dose of hysterics. Helen Bettle went across the saloon with unaccustomed quickness and helped Miss Singlestar quiet her, while Barlowe and John were both standing belligerently over the sullen-sitting Peter, and Barlowe was shouting disagreeable things loudly at Peter, at the top of his lungs.

Bettle was watching it all with an abstract bewilderment, and Wharton said: "My dear Valcour, I have a profound admiration for your methods. You simply stand quite still and permit people to explode, one by one, in proper order, around you."

Barlowe had stopped shouting at Peter; he was shouting at Valcour: "You must listen to me, Valcour. I insist that you hear what I have to say. You must listen, I tell you."

"I am," Valcour said.

"Very well then—*shut up, Freda!*—I'll tell you who those two people were."

There was quiet again. Even Freda was quiet, her weeping suddenly dried by the shock of that sudden "shut up."

Valcour said: "Who were they, please?" Barlowe's pressure dropped as rapidly as it had risen, and his face was gray sand that is damp from a receding tide. He said: "Carlotta Balfé was one of them."

"How do you know, Mr. Barlowe?"

"Because the other one was myself."

"Darling,"—Freda's voice was quite sound again—"I think you're a liar, too."

CHAPTER THIRTY-EIGHT

HEDGLIN WAS KILLED IN THIS WAY

Barlowe said: "You must appreciate the darkness, Mr. Valcour—how vague things were in general, in the darkness of the boat deck." He went back and sat down again beside Freda, and her hand was warm and tight in his cold big one, and his mind was flooded suddenly with innumerable wanted things, all revolving about a decent security, and any one of which would have made a perfect lithograph. He ended: "Quite indistinguishable."

"That's all right, Mr. Barlowe," Valcour said. "But there's one little point that I do wish you'd be good enough to clear up for me."

"Anything—anything, Mr. Valcour." (He *owned* that hand, that firm, hot, honest little hand. It was Ella's and his. Part of their own flesh and blood. God rest her—Ella…)

"Mr. Barlowe, you were seen by the first officer leaving the wireless room just a short while before a cigarette butt was found by Mr. Bettle in the operator's souvenir ashtray. Did you place that butt in the tray?"

"Lord, no."

"What were you doing in the wireless room, please?"

Barlowe looked hot. "I think you know, Mr. Valcour," he said stiltedly, "what I was doing."

Valcour glanced at his watch. Almost an hour of the four that was left them had gone by. He looked thoughtfully at Barlowe. At Barlowe and Freda. There was such a close-knittedness about the two of them, such a blending, a surging of each other through gripped hands. Her face was a white camellia capped with copper, and his eyes were those of a whipped but defiant dog. Valcour felt he knew what Barlowe had been doing in the wireless room. Barlowe had been looking through the duplicates for some written message which might involve his past. Valcour said: "Did anyone else come in while you were there? Did you meet anyone as you left?"

"No, Mr. Valcour."

"Thank you."

Barlowe's eyes weren't defiant any more. He mumbled: "That's all?"
"That is all."

Helen said tranquilly: "Aren't you going to ask him what he was do-ing? I'd like to know. When people speak about a thing they know about before me, and don't tell me what it is, it bothers me. I think about it all day." She said again: "I'd like to know." Valcour said: "Mr. Barlowe was looking up a reference to a message, Mrs. Bettle, that has no con-nection with this case."

"Thank you, Mr. Valcour. That is all I wanted to know."

Wharton was suddenly stiff in his chair. His voice was without cyni-cism. He said sharply: "Do you mean that, my dear Valcour?"

"Mean what, Mr. Luke?"

"That the message you referred to has no connection with this case?"

"I do."

Wharton noticeably joined the group of the desperately pale. He said quietly: "Then the alternative is rather drastic, isn't it?"

"Very."

"I suppose,"—Wharton was staring earnestly at Valcour; his eyes were naked-looking, and his voice fumbled—"I suppose there is no way of—"

"None, Mr. Luke. Surely you can see that for yourself?"

"Yes, I can see it."

"I wish," Helen said, "you two would tell me what you're talking about."

"I should like to give you," Valcour said quietly, "a picture, a time outline, of the Hedglin crime. Let us start at exactly nine o'clock of the evening we sailed. Mr. Moore has told me that the ship's bell was strik-ing just as he and Mr. Hedglin stepped onto the deck. They were met by Burke, who took their bags, and led them to their cabins. Burke dropped you first in yours, Mr. Moore, didn't he?"

"Yes, Mr. Valcour."

"Then you closed your cabin door and stayed there until consider-ably later? Until Miss Barlowe opened your door, having mistaken your cabin for hers?"

"Yes, Mr. Valcour."

"We have Burke, after leaving Mr. Moore, taking Mr. Hedglin to his cabin and racking his bags. Burke left Mr. Hedglin. It was then about five minutes after nine. Mr. Hedglin did not stay in his cabin. He had something to attend to at once, something urgently pressing. He went out again into the passage and either there, or in that person's cabin, met the person who was shortly to kill him."

Helen was feeling a little sick—frightened and sick. She thought: *I don't want him to say that person's name.* She drew her chair closer to Anthony's. She was closer to him than she had been in years. She felt closer to him than she had ever felt before. She wondered whether it would startle him if she were to take his hand in her hand, as Mr. Barlowe had taken one of Freda's in his. She could not remember ever having held hands.

Valcour said: "Mr. Hedglin requested this person to come at once into his, Hedglin's, cabin. It was not a pleasant scene that took place there. It could not have been entirely unpainful for Mr. Hedglin, and it must have been overwhelmingly shocking for his companion. Mr. Hedglin was producing certain papers, in the nature of a report, from his briefcase. I am still unfamiliar as to what they were, but I do know that they were sufficiently packed with dynamite to have caused Mr. Hedglin's death. I telephoned to your uncle's doctor, Mr. Moore."

"Yes, Mr. Valcour?"

"Yes. Dr. Andrew informed me that Mr. Hedglin had a weak heart, and that a wound or blow which would be insufficient to kill a man in good physical condition might quite easily kill Mr. Hedglin. That blow was struck suddenly, impulsively, in, I feel quite certain, a moment of temporary madness. It was struck with the first weapon that came to hand, with the water carafe from the rack above the basin. The blow was not sufficient to break the carafe, but it was sufficient to kill Mr. Hedglin. It was struck, I think, on the back of the skull, causing a small abrasion of the skin and a little loss of blood. The water was spilled from the carafe, and puddled the cabin rug."

Bettle said ponderously, stupidly: "There was water on the rug."

Valcour stared at him intently. "Yes, Mr. Bettle. There was water on the rug. It isn't difficult to follow what happened from then on, the returning sanity, a clearing of fogs, and the bewildering, shaking realization of what had been done. Animals, when they're trapped, think most clearly. So do men. I think the first lucid fact that was realized was that Mr. Hedglin wore a wig."

Helen was dreadfully placid about it. She said: "We've known Mr. Hedglin for a good many years. We would have known if he had worn a wig." She added inconsequentially: "It must have been a very good one."

Bettle said heavily: "Waverly told me when I first met him that he wore a wig. He knew my views concerning deceptions."

Helen said: "Yes, dear," and Wharton's voice was quieter almost than the stillness, saying: "Little sister." Helen turned and stared at him slowly. For over forty years Wharton hadn't called her that. She remembered the last time quite distinctly. She had been outgrowing dolls, and her last one had fallen from a window and shattered on the pavement. She hadn't wanted to outgrow dolls in just that way. It suddenly struck her that Wharton did know things, that his trouble was (she was lucently clear on the point) that he knew things too well.

Valcour said: "The blow and the fall, you see, had disarranged the wig, and the natural reaction was to think of disguise. The thought process is simple: *I will put on that wig, that overcoat and muffler, and that hat. I will conceal this body temporarily on the yacht. I will take this briefcase with its dangerous contents and go ashore. It will displace the scene of the crime to the city. It will end by becoming an unsolved disappearance, because when we are out at sea I will throw the body over the side.*"

Wharton said: "Aren't you being a bit omniscient, my dear Valcour?"

"I don't think so, Mr. Luke. I'm building this picture on obvious deductions from clear facts. We know that the carafe was refilled with tap water, wiped clear of fingerprints, and replaced in the rack. We know that, by that time, the simplicity of the man's intention was elaborated with essential details. He wanted the yacht, you see, to sail. It had to sail, or otherwise he would have almost insurmountable difficulties in disposing of the body. He wanted the sailing to take place as it had originally been planned, with no immediate search instituted for Mr. Hedglin, with no inquiries being made about Mr. Hedglin. This required some plausible explanation being invented for Mr. Hedglin's sudden giving up of the cruise. So he wrote a note, the one which was delivered to Mr. Bettle, and wiped the typewriter keys clear of prints. He was almost feverishly impressed with attention to details by then. Those things are facts, not omniscience. Miss Singlestar's assertion that the arm of the body she came upon in the wicker chair slid with a curious slowness down along the side of the chair establishes that death occurred about half-past nine. The curious slowness was simply rigor mortis moving downward from the head."

Miss Singlestar said: "I don't think I can stand this."

"Would you prefer going to your cabin?"

"I don't think I could, Mr. Valcour."

"There's no objection to it, Miss Singlestar."

"If I went out on deck?"

"Certainly."

They watched her, walking nervously toward the door, fumbling with its handle, leaving them, closing the door. Valcour said: "It was necessary to be in two places at once: to go ashore disguised as Mr. Hedglin, and still to remain on the yacht. Burke was employed for establishing an alibi on the yacht. The man returned to his own cabin and rang for Burke. He told Burke that he did not wish to be disturbed. He then was faced with the necessity of concealing Mr. Hedglin's body until it could be permanently disposed of at sea." Valcour took something from his pocket. "This," he said, "is a sliver of wood. There is blood on it."

Peter said stiffly: "I thought the chair was wicker?"

"This isn't from a chair, Mr. Moore. It's from a cabin locker."

Helen said: "And all of the time he must have known what was in the locker."

"All of the time."

CHAPTER THIRTY-NINE

THE MURDERER DID THESE THINGS

Valcour said: "There are several other things we can gather without omniscience. We know that the man must have approximated Mr. Hedglin's height, or the overcoat would have looked peculiar. He must have been reasonably strong, enough so to have carried Hedglin's body into his cabin and locked it in his locker; later to have carried it out on deck and set it in the armchair when Miss Singlestar's unexpected appearance disturbed him; then, after she had gone, to have lowered it over the side. It's from such things that we build our pictures. Well, the note is written, the body is concealed, and an alibi has been established through Burke. All that took time. About half an hour. That brings us up to half-past nine. It was around then that Carlotta Balfé went out on deck and sat in a chair from where the accommodation ladder was plainly visible."

Bettle said: "Carlotta. I miss Carlotta."

Helen did take his hand. It was very loose, very limp. She said: "Yes, dear." It cost her something to add: 'We all of us miss her, dear."

Valcour went on: "The forged signature on the note is an additional link in our chain of tangible evidence. The man was intensely worried about circumstantial evidence. He searched Mr. Hedglin's luggage rapidly but carefully. He made the cabin quite orderly, with the exception of his repacking of the bags. There was no time for that. Things were just stuffed back in, and the bags closed. It is interesting to note that, having access to Hedglin's keys, he did not lock the bags. I believe that the body had been placed in the locker by that time, and that the man rather dreaded approaching it again. To get the keys. The man put on Mr. Hedglin's wig."

Helen said placidly: "I don't see how he could bring himself to do that. Of everything else, I think I should have most hated doing that."

"He had to, Mrs. Bettle. The wig, and the muffler well up about his chin, the overcoat, and the hat. He then took the briefcase and the note he had prepared and went out on deck. It must have shocked him to see Carlotta Balfé sitting there. She waved to him. He did not wave back.

He hurried down the accommodation ladder and into the tender. He purposely exposed the wig to the sailor in the tender, to establish the gray hair. When they reached the yacht-club wharf he gave the note to the sailor to take back with him to the yacht. He again exposed the wig, this time to the wharf watchman, while waiting for a taxicab to be called."

Freda was staring with dreadful intensity at Peter. She was thinking: *He's tall and big and strong.* She disliked vigorously the absolute knowledge of the fact that, if he wanted her to, she would marry him that minute.

Valcour said: "The rest is rather obvious routine. The man gave the taxi driver an address in the theater district, as the easiest place to escape unnoticed from the cab. He left the hat and overcoat in the cab, so that the police would identify them as Mr. Hedglin's and conclude that Mr. Hedglin had disappeared in the city. He carried the wig and briefcase with him, got out of the cab, vanished in the theater-district crowd, took another taxi, and was driven back to the neighborhood of the yacht-club wharf. That carries us up to about ten-thirty." Valcour said directly to Freda: "You boarded the yacht with Miss Singlestar shortly after then, Miss Barlowe, didn't you?"

"Yes, Mr. Valcour." Freda added thoughtfully: "Why?"

"Nothing in particular. I wondered whether you noticed any rowboat on your way from the wharf to the yacht."

"No."

"Because the man used a rowboat; one he had stolen from a neighboring wharf. He removed the papers from the briefcase and probably tore them up, then threw them in the river. He didn't throw the wig in the river because he was afraid it would float, which it would have, and be found. He carried that back on board with him when he climbed up by means of the anchor chain."

"My dear Valcour," Wharton said, "this ceases to be omniscience. It is second-sight."

"Not at all, Mr. Luke. The man got his trouser legs wet while doing it."

"But I still insist on necromancy."

"He got his trouser legs wet, and later stole the steward's electric iron to press them out with. The trouble is, he met Carlotta Balfé as he was on the way to his cabin."

"She saw the wet legs?"

"What is more important, Mr. Luke, he *knew* that she saw the wet legs." Valcour said directly to Peter: "Mr. Moore, it is perfectly true that you did see a woman on the boat deck just before the wireless man was struck, but it wasn't Miss Barlowe. It was Carlotta Balfé."

Peter was a reddening stone, staring transfixed at Freda. It occurred to him vaguely that she was sticking her tongue out at him. Helen Bettle, with placid astonishment, was observing the tongue, too. She thought: *Things must be different at Miss Ketcham's than they were in my day*. Perhaps it wasn't Miss Ketcham's, but simply that the times had changed. People were constantly telling her so. Every similar year. Helen couldn't see it. People got to places quicker and more comfortably, but that was all. They still did about the same things and thought the same thoughts when they got to them. Freda stuck her tongue out. In Helen's day it would have been a frozen "look." But the inherent purpose of the gestures was identical. Helen still mildly preferred the frozen look, especially in a prospective daughter-in-law…daughter-in-law… John *had* proposed to Freda and Freda had accepted him…not over ten minutes ago…those dreadful and violent tears…

Wharton was saying: "Who was the man with Carlotta Balfé, my dear Valcour?"

And Valcour was saying: "Her murderer."

CHAPTER FORTY

"CRUSADER" LABORS FRETFULLY

Bettle's voice was startling. Heavy, forceful, and like a strong sure wind. He was suddenly fuller and quite confident again in himself. He took his hand with abstract impatience from Helen's. He said: "Mr. Valcour, that statement is incorrect. Carlotta Balfé was not killed by a mortal."

Helen thought: *It doesn't work*. This holding of hands. It didn't matter very much. Nothing could matter very much after twenty-five years of close living with a person. Matter *suddenly*. It was stupid to think it could. A good many things were becoming very plain to Helen. If you married a man for his money it was stupid to expect that twenty-five years later he would find any pleasure or reason for holding your hand. She also thought, with soothing triteness: *It's better to have just a little money of your own, and do something that really matters with it, than to have lots of money and do lots of things with it that don't matter at all.* Even if the pennies just bought bread. Her head was beginning to ache badly. She had discovered during the past twenty-five years that it was bad for her to think. She decided to stop. She said to Anthony: "But she was stabbed, dear."

Wharton said with deliberate bitterness: "My brother-in-law is implying, dear Helen, that the hands which can tip a table can also wield a knife."

"I doubt," Valcour said, "that they would adjust the hands of a watch. Mr. Bettle, it won't work. Carlotta Balfé was killed for the plain and human reason that she knew very well that her murderer had killed Mr. Hedglin. I don't think she knew why he had killed Mr. Hedglin, any more than I do."

Wharton said sharply: "You are ignorant of the motive?"

"Quite."

"Then your case would be rather shaky in a court of law."

"Very shaky, Mr. Luke. All homicide cases based on circumstantial evidence are."

"And if you will permit me to point it out, my dear Valcour, such circumstantial evidence as you do possess is extraordinarily flimsy."

Helen thought: *Wharton is working for something. Whenever he sits tightly like that, like pressed springs, he's working for something.*

"If you care to look at it that way, Mr. Luke," Valcour said.

"How else can we? How else will a jury? You have nothing but a plausible fabrication of what you call the Hedglin crime. You've a water-wetted rug that is now dry. You can't offer that as a very convincing exhibit to a jury. You've a fingerprintless carafe—fingerprintless on your own testimony and nobody else's—which has probably been smashed during the recent storm. God knows, almost everything else has been. You've a typewriter with its keys wiped off. It may not be plausible, but it certainly is possible that Hedglin wiped them off himself. You've a signature which you claim is forged. I don't have to point out to you how flatly contradictory the testimony of opposing experts in court can be. You've a little square of wicker and a sliver of wood, both of which may be minutely stained with what you claim is blood. You haven't even Hedglin's body. You haven't one single decisive proof that he is dead. All pretty slender, my dear Valcour." Valcour smiled faintly. "So slender, Mr. Luke, as to be, in themselves, absurd."

"You are deliberately fishing for a confession."

Valcour's smile broadened. "Of what?"

"I know. That shows I do believe a crime has taken place, but I do not yield one inch. I am pointing out what a jury will believe and not what I think myself." Wharton said with almost exaggerated distinctness: "Without a confession, my dear Valcour, no jury on earth would convict."

Valcour looked at his watch. There was a sluggish feeling about the motion of the yacht. It seemed to him that she did not lift through the waves with her natural buoyancy any longer, but was laboring fretfully. He wondered whether Captain Jorgensen had included the probable reduction in speed due to the increasing weight of the water in her hold in his calculations for a junction point of the *Crusader* and the *Eastern Coast*. He wondered what plans had been made for the transfer of Carlotta's body. It shouldn't be done hideously, strapped with torn sheets to a bed. He said: "We do have a corpus delicti in the case of Carlotta Balfé, Mr. Luke. We have a motive, too."

"We have a problematic motive, my dear Valcour, and not one atom of circumstantial proof. You haven't even the weapon. I repeat strenuously that without a confession both crimes will remain legally unsolved."

Helen thought: *I've never seen Wharton perspire before.*

Valcour was saying: "Let me continue with the picture as I see it, Mr. Luke. We come to the disposal of Mr. Hedglin's body. There are two interesting details in that whole business. One is that the murderer put the wig back on Mr. Hedglin's head before dropping the body over the side. It points to certain innate decencies of breeding. It gives an insight into the complex character of the man. Don't you agree?"

"Either that or a Teutonic sense of orderliness."

Helen thought: *Wharton is saying words emptily.*

"The other detail," Valcour said, "is convincing proof to me that Carlotta Balfé was certain that the Hedglin crime had been committed, and knew its perpetrator. She took her handkerchief and wiped the blood spot from the wicker chair and then dropped her handkerchief over the side. I am frankly puzzled about that message she believed she had received from her control Maybelle. I am puzzled in this sense: I do not disbelieve, in crucial moments of one's life, in psychic manifestations. I cannot disbelieve in them. The fact that the ordinary run of them have been capitalized by charlatans has nothing to do with it. There are too many authenticated instances that have occurred in great, in tense, crises, when hidden senses are peculiarly receptive, when they are able (these senses) to break through the covering of disuse which has all but atrophied them—there are too many such instances to make disbelief anything but willful stupidity. Whether that message was spoken by the eavesdropping murderer or by Carlotta herself, regardless of its wording or import, I think it was a genuine psychic manifestation, a warning to her that she stood, as she did stand, close in the face of death."

Bettle said: "Yes. Very close. Quite close in the face of death."

"The mechanics of the attack on Mr. Meddletree were simple to follow," Valcour said. "The man wished to overhear my telephone conversation with the commissioner. He heard me requesting Mr. Meddletree to stay in his sleeping quarters. He hid himself at once in the cabin locker, watched Mr. Meddletree, and struck him when Mr. Meddletree had his back turned and his ear pressed against the connecting door. He remained in the locker during my talk with Meddletree, while Meddletree was coming to, and left the cabin when Meddletree went back into the wireless room to turn off the set."

"And why do you place him in the sleeping quarters both before the operator went into them, and until after you and he had left them?" Wharton asked.

"Because the deck door of that cabin, Mr. Luke, has a noisy hinge. Mr. Meddletree would have heard it opening. And therefore the man was already inside. He did not leave immediately after young Meddletree was struck because he wanted to overhear my talk with the commissioner, which he did."

"For any special reason?"

"To learn whether Mr. Hedglin had told him the truth when Mr. Hedglin had said, to this man, that there were no duplicates of the report that was in the briefcase in his office, and that no one knew of its existence but Mr. Hedglin himself."

"This is pure and rather dangerous romance."

"It is a negative deduction. The man would never have killed Mr. Hedglin unless he felt certain that Mr. Hedglin alone knew the contents of that report, unless it was simply a delaying gesture, and I don't believe it was."

"These statements are quite untenable in court."

"Quite."

"So that apart from an outright confession, which I say again you are deliberately fishing for, your case has the baffling and futile consistency of a patch of fog."

Valcour was staring thoughtfully at the deck door, watching it open, watching young Meddletree come in with a message blank in his hand. "You seem to have forgotten, Mr. Luke," he said, "that almost the entire police force of New York City is working on this case ashore."

CHAPTER FORTY-ONE

SAILORS TAKE DOORS

Valcour took the message blank from young Meddletree, who said : "I've got to hurry. I've got to hurry right back, Mr. Valcour. You know."

"Everything going all right?"

"Yes, sir. All right. Meet in thirty minutes. I got to hurry…"

Meddletree was gone, and Valcour examined the message blank. Its code was the same as the one he had sent. He was able, from practice, to read it at a glance.

Helen said tranquilly: "Meet what? What is it that meets in thirty minutes? My head is aching and I don't feel very well." And Wharton was pressing one of her hands. She felt as startled as Anthony must have felt when she had taken one of his. Only Anthony hadn't felt startled, really. He hadn't felt one way or the other about it at all. She thought: *Nice habits which young people go in for never do grow old. They never tarnish. They never lose their clean and pleasant polish with old age.* She suddenly felt herself clinging to Wharton's smooth and overwarm hand as if it were an anchor against something. Against a towering and unseen wave. Against (she thought: *I might as well admit it*) panic.

Valcour was folding and refolding the message, absently twisting it between his fingers, circling with thoughtful eyes the people in the saloon, observing Freda and Barlowe with their aching stillness, and Peter, hot, red, and alone, and John and Anthony and Helen Bettle, with Wharton like a neat white sword of flame between his sister, between his sister and her little aches and pains, between her feeble tentacles on the happinesses of life, and… "Even in a carefully premeditated crime," Valcour said, "there are slips. In an inspirational one such as the killing of Mr. Hedglin, there were bound to be slips. This message from the police commissioner tells me of two. They occurred in the city. One was of the man's own volition, and the other one was beyond his control. There are, in addition, two others. They were both of the man's own volition and occurred on this yacht. I have said nothing of them as yet."

Very neat, very white, like a sword of flame… "You do not dare name this man, Valcour," Wharton said. "You know that you are fishing in dangerous waters. You know the heavy penalty that can be exacted for such a drastic, such a false, accusation."

Valcour said wearily: "I'm not afraid, Mr. Luke. It's true that I'm waiting for a confession, and if it will make you feel any better I'll admit that I will wait for one right up to the last. A confession not only aids the State, but it relieves the minds of those who are interested in the criminal's welfare that there has been no miscarriage of justice. The police are in possession of the motive of this crime. I know all about it now. I know each one of its little, tragic, pitiful, and cheap details."

Wharton pounced on the significant word. "Cheap?"

"Very cheap, Mr. Luke. I don't think I have to point out to you Mr. Bettle's character. You all know him for what he is: a fanatically sincere and inexorable man."

Bettle said with shocked and angry forcefulness: "I object to your use of the term 'fanatical,' Mr. Valcour."

"Perhaps because we do not both read into it the same meaning, Mr. Bettle."

"I object to it in any sense."

"Which further proves my contention. You are a man, Mr. Bettle, who is living in a very tight and private room."

"You are being both offensive and absurd."

"I am being neither. Your great wealth has made you, as it does with nine men out of ten, an egomaniac. It is a distinct and an unpleasant experience when somebody disagrees with you. The rareness of it creates a shock. You are a good man, a sincere man, an honest man. And you are an egomaniac. You feel yourself superior to your contemporaries and to government. You are like a man on a self-established pinnacle that is so high that he feels he has leveled himself with God."

"You are being sacrilegious."   "I am interpreting correctly your own purposes and actions. What are you doing? What have you done? You've said to yourself: *Liquor and tobacco are two evil things. Neither mankind nor its governments can do anything about it, no matter how hard they have tried. Their laws, their great investigation committees, have been a futile farce. But I can do something. I will get together with God and we'll do something about it. Money, you have said to yourself, is the securest weapon on earth. It is blindly obedient and it cannot betray. I have lots of money. What a monument I can build with it for myself if I use it for stamping out the liquor and tobacco evils on earth.*" Valcour was dreadfully tired. He said: "Doesn't it seem a little silly and childish, Mr. Bettle, when it's put that way?"

Bettle said: "The devil himself is a sophist."

"All right. Take your actions. Take the results of this mania, this hobby which has obsessed you. For the past two or three years it has been an increasingly consuming growth inside of you, nourishing itself on your normally sane outlook on life and the world about you."

"Mr. Valcour, this is hysterical nonsense."

"Hysterical if you wish, but not nonsense. Unless you care to consider the murders of Hedglin and Carlotta Balfé as nonsense."

"You are trying to tell me that my plans had anything to do with them?"

"You are your plans. They give us a reading of you."

"It is you who are the fanatic, Mr. Valcour. You are insane. You are tired. You have overworked your nerves with all of this. You are insane."

Helen said: "Yes, dear Anthony. You mustn't worry. Things happen anyway."

"Your plans, Mr. Bettle," Valcour went on, "are a portrait of yourself. Their very elaborateness and mass of detail. Their assumption of the Germanic idea of a pyramidal trust. Your decision to fight the devil with evil, to use as we of the police use—you pointed this out to me yourself—the strategy of having agents planted behind the enemy lines. If my words are grandiloquent it is because your plans were grandiloquent—this decision of yours to start at the bottom by establishing the most far-reaching organization that the illicit liquor trade has ever known, to accumulate the positive and conclusive proofs of all the trade's ramifications, its essential briberies and corruptions, to accumulate them as no government-appointed commission ever could. Your plan for one death-dealing expose that would hold up, for the entire nation to see, every proven ugliness of this cancerous growth. Your plans, your purpose, your integrity, your positive assurance in your own rightness are, Mr. Bettle, magnificent. Your trouble lies in your tight and private room. You don't know the living word. You don't know your fellow men. All you really do know is a couple of ideas that you think might be good for them."

"Your opinions do not interest me, Mr. Valcour. Nor this digression."

"It isn't a digression. Hedglin and Carlotta Balfé were killed for the plain reason that you're what you are."

Wharton said with unconcealed nervousness: "May I bring you back to the problematic jury again, my dear Valcour? You speak of slips. May we know what they are?"

"Certainly, Mr. Luke. This message from headquarters tells me that there has been an identification."

Helen thought: *Wharton's hand is squeezing painfully hard, but it doesn't hurt me.*

Wharton was obviously dumfounded. "An identification? Made ashore?"

"Yes. You see, the man did take another taxicab back to the vicinity of the yacht-club wharf. He shouldn't have. He should either have taken a street car or, if he felt that he had the time, have walked. You must remember that by then he was hatless, coatless, and carried the briefcase. The wig was in his pocket. He had become, in other words, conspicuous, considering the coldness of the night. We do not realize, aboard here, the tremendous amount of publicity which the newspapers have been giving to this case in the city. The taxi driver who drove the murderer back to the yacht logically connected the hatless, coatless man and the briefcase with the Hedglin disappearance and reported his suspicions to headquarters. He even remembered seeing what struck him as a wig sticking out of one of the man's pockets. He gave headquarters a very good description of the man. It's here in this message. It's very good."

Wharton said in the deathlike stillness: "And the other slip?"

"Mr. Hedglin did leave in his office some scrapped notes on the dangerous report. His stenographer was finally persuaded to give them to the police. Even in their fragmentary state they are sufficient to point the motive clearly."

Two sailors and Miss Singlestar came hurriedly in from the deck. They started (the sailors) to remove the saloon doors from their hinges.

Helen said placidly: "Why are these men taking off the doors?"

Miss Singlestar found difficulty in speaking. She said: "They are building rafts. I think we're about to sink."

CHAPTER FORTY-TWO

BULLET

Valcour kept a hand in his coat pocket, and fingers of the hand were closed about the butt of a gun. Lifebelts were ungainly on the assembled people, lining the starboard rail, watching the bobbing boats that were coming toward them over a strip of intervening deep blue water from the *Eastern Coast*.

The yacht had settled dangerously deep, with tired and heavy bows. She was stripped, and gaunt, and old, and seemed thirstily eager for the final cooling closing-over of the waters that would hide her bone-picked nakedness and give her decent burial in private chambers of the all-securing sea.

Valcour stood apart with Bettle, very alert, very watchful, his fingers in constant contact with the gun. Bettle was in a thorough and ice-cold rage. His voice was bitterly quiet and held harsh edges. He said: "I did not think you were a stupid man, Mr. Valcour."

"No, Mr. Bettle?"

"No. Your deliberate linking of these crimes with myself is inexcusably stupid. There was, if you wish, a certain privacy in regard to the report in Hedglin's briefcase, but there was no secrecy. I already knew all there was to know about Horatio Barlowe. I knew all about his wife, about Freda's mother. That business of her having been a pickpocket was an inexcusably shocking error on the part of Carlotta. Mrs. Barlowe was in all senses a very fine woman, who had the misfortune to find herself not only married to but in love with a swindler. Hedglin's investigation of Barlowe's past was simply a check-up to reassure ourselves that we were correct. A man who had had no contact, no working knowledge of the principles of evil, would have been unsuitable to me. Barlowe knew that I knew all about him over an hour before Hedglin set foot, even, on the yacht. Barlowe isn't an idiot. He's a very smart man. He wouldn't kill a man to prevent something from becoming known which he knew was already known."

"I'm sure he wouldn't. I don't think he'd ever kill anybody for any reason, Mr. Bettle. Swindlers don't."

Bettle was shocked into complete attention. "Then what are you driving at?"

"The report I was speaking about did not concern Mr. Barlowe."

"Whom did it concern?"

"The murderer."

Bettle stared thoughtfully at Valcour. "I'm beginning to change my opinion about you again," he said. Bettle's stare moved slowly downward. "There's a gun in your pocket and your hand is on it. Why?"

Valcour glanced at bobbing boats, large white flakes on the deep blue waters. "Something might happen during the transfer," he said.

The first of the four boats was very close, showing the features of her rowers, brick bronze in a westering sun, of an officer in her sheets, a big, clean, muscled-looking man in white duck trousers and a white shirt opened at an impressive neck. He was calling something to Captain Jorgensen, and Captain Jorgensen was being very businesslike in his calling back.

"Tell me, Mr. Valcour," Bettle said quietly, "the nature of that report."

"Mr. Bettle, can you recall with any accuracy how you felt when you found that cigarette butt in the wireless man's ashtray?"

"Certainly. It was inexcusable."

"It was symbolic, wasn't it—the cigarette butt—of your deeply rooted opinion concerning tobacco and drink, which are in turn simply symbols of dissipation, or of evil living?"

Bettle thought about this. "You are quite right."

"In other words, it is the principle underlying an offense rather than the mildness or the greatness of the offense itself which counts with you, isn't it?"

"It is."

The women were boarding the *Eastern Coast*'s first boat. Freda, Miss Singlestar, the stewardess, and Helen Bettle. Four sailors were waiting to place Carlotta's body (surprisingly little-looking in its satin cover) in the sheets.

Valcour said: "You would never condone, and could never forgive."

Bettle was quite honest. "I would never under any circumstances condone. I don't think I could ever forgive. It would not be in my province to do so."

Valcour thought: *He is back again, with God.* He said: "That's what the man knew. That's why, in sudden shock and fright, in a mental bewilderment that approached madness, he killed Hedglin. To suppress that report. He killed Carlotta Balfé because she knew he had killed Hedglin and because she was using her knowledge to blackmail him into a marriage. That theatrical dummy business in her bed was not simply because she was fundamentally a theatrical person. She wanted to be absolutely certain that she was correct. She was deliberately baiting the man to come in and attempt to murder her. That would so very finally have wiped out any possibility of a denial on his part."

Bettle said: "I have never wanted to kill anyone, Mr. Valcour, but I think I could kill that man. I want you to tell me who he is. You will tell me, please, why you are so certain of your grounds, and you will tell me who he is."

Valcour said quietly, distinctly: "He is a poor fellow human being, Mr. Bettle, who sowed one little wild oat."

Bettle's face changed slowly, as the sky does when light leaves it to the evening. He said: "The symbol." And: "When did you know?"

"When it came to me that the coastal stations would never have issued a fair-weather report in the teeth of a hurricane. When I realized that the message given to me in regard to Peter Moore would neither have been worded as it was nor have come to me at all except in code."

Bettle's voice was thinned into the quiet air.

"The message that was given to you by—"

"Your son."

"We are ready, gentlemen. There is no hurry, but I shall ask you to be quick." Captain Jorgensen was a bluff and businesslike wind. He bustled Bettle, unresisting, to the accommodation ladder. Valcour went, too. They went down to the waiting boat.

John was in the boat. John, and Peter, and Wharton, and Barlowe. Valcour stepped into the boat and sat between Bettle and his son. Great oars dipped in the deep blue waters. The yacht receded gently as they headed for the *Eastern Coast*.

It was midway between the two ships that John jumped. His plunge was deep and carried him out of sight entirely, and when he came up again his face was a polished gray fleck on the deep blue waters. The boat moved cumbersomely in confusion, and Valcour, balancing precariously, drew his gun.

The officer in the stern sheets said sharply: "What's the idea?" He followed Valcour's shocked stare. He said: "Good God!"

Slick and lazy and ugly, the shark was, and its belly flashed a dirty white in the setting sun.

"Steady with your aim, man!" the officer said.

There was no breathing in the boat, and Valcour fired. It was a gentle sound, that *crack*, in the quiet immensity of the ocean, and Valcour never knew whether it had been willfully done or not. The little joggle that Bettle had given to his arm.

ABOUT RUFUS KING

Rufus King (1893–1966) was an American author of Whodunit crime novels. He created four series of detective stories: the first one with Reginald De Puyster, a sophisticated detective similar to Philo Vance; the second one with his more famous character, Lieutenant Valcour; Colin Starr, who appeared in four stories in the *Strand Magazine* during 1940/41; and Detective Bill Duggan, who appeared in three stories in 1956/57. The Bill Duggan stories include his most famous short work, "Malice in Wonderland" (which loaned its title to his 1958 hardcover short story collection).

Modern critics are rediscovering Rufus King's work. Mike Grost, on *Golden Age Detective*, features a long writeup of King, stating: "King had a vivid writing style, with colorful characters, events, and images. He was clearly a born writer."